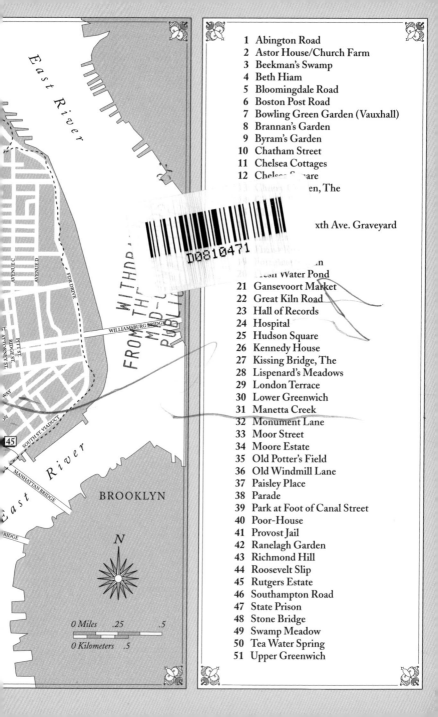

East River

East River

WILLIAMSBURG BRIDGE

MANHATTAN BRIDGE

BROOKLYN

45

SOUTH ST. VIADUCT

FDR DRIVE

AVENUE C

AVENUE D

PITT ST

RIDGE ST

ATTORNEY ST

WITHDRAWN FROM THE MID-CONTINENT PUBLIC

N

| 0 Miles | .25 | .5 |

| 0 Kilometers | .5 |

# IN OLD NEW YORK

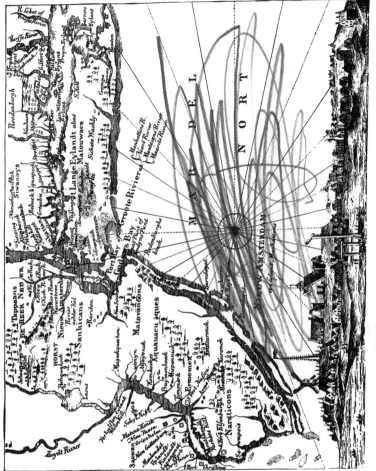

MAP OF NEW NETHERLANDS—With a view of New Amsterdam (now New York), A.D. 1656

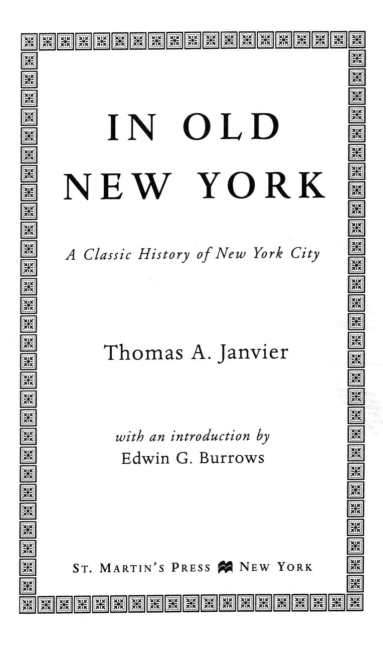

# IN OLD
# NEW YORK

*A Classic History of New York City*

## Thomas A. Janvier

*with an introduction by*
Edwin G. Burrows

ST. MARTIN'S PRESS ⚓ NEW YORK

IN OLD NEW YORK. Copyright © 1894 by Harper &
Brothers. Copyright © renewed 1922 by Mrs.
Catharine A. Janvier. Introduction copyright © 2000
by Edwin Burrows. All rights reserved. Printed in the
United States of America. No part of this book may
be used or reproduced in any manner whatsoever
without written permission except in the case of brief
quotations embodied in critical articles or reviews.
For information, address St. Martin's Press, 175 Fifth
Avenue, New York, N.Y. 10010.

ISBN 0-312-24282-4

First published in the United States under the title
*In Old New York* by Harper & Brothers

First St. Martin's Press Edition: April 2000

10 9 8 7 6 5 4 3 2 1

TO

C. A. J.

# CONTENTS

# ILLUSTRATIONS

# ILLUSTRATIONS

# MAPS

———

# INTRODUCTION

*IN OLD NEW YORK*, first published by Harper & Brothers in 1894, was the tenth of some twenty books written by Thomas A. Janvier during a long literary career and the first of three excursions he would make into the history of New York City (*The Dutch Founding of New York* followed in 1903 and *Henry Hudson* in 1909, both also published by Harper). Still prized by students of the city's past, it is arguably his best work and—although out of print for many years now—the only one for which he is likely to be remembered today.

Like many New York historians before and since, Thomas Allibone Janvier had been lured to the city from somewhere else—in his case, Philadelphia, where he was born in 1849 to an old Huguenot family with a passion for literature. His father published verse, his mother wrote stories for children, and his older sister, Margaret, would achieve modest fame as the author of poems, stories, and novels for young adults. Not surprisingly, young Thomas, too, yearned to be a writer and in 1871 embarked on a career in journalism with a succession of Philadelphia newspapers. In 1878, closing in on his thirtieth birthday, he married Catharine Ann Drinker, an instructor at the Pennsylvania Academy of the Fine Arts who was making a name for herself as a painter. Philadelphia could not contain the Janviers, however. Restless, inquisitive, and enamored of the exotic, they left on a three-year tour of the American West and Mexico. No one who knew them could have been surprised that when they finally came back to the East in 1884 they chose to settle in Greenwich Village.

By the mid-1880s, though the Village's glory days as the axis of American nonconformity lay a decade or two in the future, the concentration of avant-garde writers and artists around Washington Square was already approaching a kind of critical mass. On the northeast corner of the square, New York University's decrepit Gothic Revival building (eventually torn down in 1894) rented rooms to Eastman Johnson, Winslow Homer, George Inness, and other prominent American painters. Just east of Sixth Avenue, in the celebrated Tenth Street Studios—the first edifice of its kind in the country—were the romantically cluttered ateliers and apartments of John La Farge, Frederick Church, William Merritt Chase, and the writer Thomas Bailey Aldrich, among others. Across the street stood the home of the Tile Club, where some of the country's most influential artists, sculptors, and architects gathered to dine and paint pictures on Spanish tiles. Not far away, either, were such bastions of art and literature as the Century Association, the National Academy of Design, and the Salmagundi Club, along with a supporting cast of quaint cafés, charming little restaurants, small hotels, and the private homes where respectable ladies and gentlemen hosted literary salons. It all seemed very Bohemian, very Parisian, very Left Bank (the area around Washington Square was often referred to as the Latin or French Quarter). The affable and cosmopolitan Janviers fit right in—especially Thomas, who was remembered by one of his editors as having "the vivacity of a Frenchman, the sturdy physical build of an Englishman, and the adaptability of an American . . . an artist of exceptional attraction . . . a very handsome creature."

Janvier soon produced a number of stories about Village characters, first published by New York magazines then collected in his first book, *Color Studies* (1885). Over the next ten years, he churned out additional novels and travel books about Mexico, Spain, and France, plus a study of current military affairs. He became a regular contributor to *Harper's Magazine,* the most widely read journal of the day, which was under the editorial leadership of Henry Mills Alden, the champion of such new American writers as William Dean Howells, Mark Twain, Henry James, Bret Harte, and Stephen Crane. He also threw himself into the study of local history for the essays that would make up *In Old New York,* haunted by the thought that time was running out on the offbeat, colorful precincts where Art found inspiration and sustenance.

Even in a city where change had long since become a way of life, Janvier's first decade in New York must have seemed unusually tumultuous. A sudden upsurge of immigrants from Russia and Italy drove the population of Manhattan from 1.2 million in 1880 to 2.0 million in 1900. (A new federal immigration station on Ellis Island opened in 1892, replacing Castle Garden on the Battery.) Little Italy and the Jewish Lower East Side, one of the most densely populated places in the world, expanded rapidly toward Greenwich Village as a new generation of urban reformers began to grapple with problems of overcrowding, crime, sanitation, and education. (The first edition of Jacob Riis's *How the Other Half Lives* appeared in 1890.) In 1886, meanwhile, a violent clash between club-wielding police and striking horsecar drivers galvanized the labor movement and set the stage for that year's three-way mayoral campaign, one of the most turbulent on record, in which the radical Henry George ran a close second. Unionists, socialists, and anarchists multiplied in the depression that followed the Panic of 1893—on one occasion Emma Goldman famously urged a crowd of thousands to loot the homes of the rich—while the Lexow Committee of 1894–95 compiled volumes of testimony confirming that vice, corruption, and racketeering were pandemic in the city. Where Janvier stood in all this commotion may be judged from his futuristic novel *The Women's Conquest of New-York,* an ostensibly tongue-in-cheek tale of how the adoption of female suffrage brought about the election of one Bridget O'Dowd as "Mayoress," shifting power to the ignorant foreign-born masses and the venal bosses who controlled them. It was published by Harper & Brothers in 1894, the same year he completed *In Old New York.*

*In Old New York* is a much more serious and good-natured book, but it too has an edge. The opening chapter lays the foundation for what follows with a careful account of New York's relentless growth up to the early nineteenth century, when the Erie Canal and railroads made it the undisputed commercial center of the United States. We do not tumble to Janvier's game until he reaches the commission chosen in 1807 to anticipate the development of Manhattan above Houston Street. Wasting this "magnificent opportunity" to create a beautiful city, he writes, "these excellently dull gentlemen" issued a plan that "was all right angles and straight lines," an unimaginative gridwork that fell far short "of what might have been accomplished by men of

genius governed by artistic taste." Yet it was not entirely the commissioners' fault, he adds, for they merely reflected "the dulness [sic] and
intense utilitarianism of the people and the period whereof they were
a part. Assuredly, the work would have been done with more dash and
spirit a whole century earlier—in the slave-dealing and piratical days
of New York, when life here had a flavor of romance in it and was not
a mere grind of money-making in stupid commonplace ways."

Of course, the notion that slavery and piracy made New York
"romantic" is ill-considered foolishness. Not at all foolish—and indeed
a major reason why *In Old New York* seems so fresh a century after its
initial publication—is Janvier's disdain for the impatient, vulgar com-
mercialism that would obliterate every trace of history in its path.
Succeeding chapters—on Greenwich Village, Lispenard's Meadows,
Love Lane, the Battery, the Debtors' Prison, Old-Time Pleasure
Gardens—play out variations on this theme as Janvier escorts his readers to places that revive the stories of people and events all but forgotten in the city's frenzied pursuit of wealth. He makes a genial guide,
too, dispensing the necessary doses of historical background with a
light touch, tossing off droll little witticisms (by taking the Abingdon
Road to the Kissing Bridge, he tells us, lovers "very agreeably prolonged the oscupontine situation"), eagerly scouting out "picturesque"
vestiges of days gone by to contrast with "the dull newness of the
advancing town." And as in his fiction and travel books, he writes with
a painter's eye for color, shape, and perspective: "The view at the head
of King Street, by-the-way—over the low wooden houses to the towering west front of the church of Sant' Antonio di Padua—at about
eleven o'clock in the morning, when is had the right effect of light and
shade, is one of the most satisfying views in New York." (Abundant
drawings by W. A. Rogers and Howard Pyle, two of the best-known
artists on the Harper payroll, add visual weight to Janvier's romantic
sensibility.)

Janvier's love of the picturesque had limits, to be sure. His scorn for
the "mere grind of money-making" was aesthetic, not political, and it
would never have occurred to him that *In Old New York* might be read
as an indictment of urban capitalist culture—not even for the relatively modest purposes of historic preservation. (Apparently he took no

part in either the fight to save City Hall from demolition in 1893 or the creation of the American Scenic and Historic Preservation Society two years later.) More telling still are Janvier's periodic outbursts of rancor against the new immigrants from eastern and central Europe. To his way of thinking, for example, Greenwich Village at the end of the nineteenth century remains a bastion of "humanity of the better sort" and offers "a liberal lesson in cleanliness, good citizenship, and self-respect—agreeably free from the foul odors and the foul humanity which make expeditions in the vicinity of Chatham Square, while abstractly delightful, so stingingly distressing to one's nose and soul." This nativist condescension was nothing if not commonplace in Janvier's day—it permeates Riis's *How the Other Half Lives*—but modern readers of *In Old New York* may well wonder why the exotic scenes and scents that stirred Janvier's imagination in, say, Mexico or France would repel him in New York. Only the almost offhand qualification—"while abstractly delightful"—suggests that he himself ever suspected an inconsistency in his opinions.

In the meantime, even as *In Old New York* began to appear in city bookstores, the Janviers were moving to a new home in the south of France. They lived there for the next three years, contentedly wining and dining with local poets and novelists, then moved to London for a stay of several additional years. The couple returned again to New York in 1900, eventually making their home at the Gainsborough Studios on Central Park South, where Thomas died in June 1913, just shy of his sixty-fourth birthday. The next year, Harper & Brothers published his last book, *At the Casa Napoleon,* a collection of short stories about the residents of a tiny hotel, just off lower Fifth Avenue, where he once entertained his literary companions.

In the preface to *Casa Napoleon,* Harper editor Ripley Hitchcock praised Janvier's work for its "mellowness and quaintness," a gentle verdict that goes a long way to explaining why the bulk of it was already falling into obscurity. Following the trail blazed by such novels as William Dean Howells's *A Hazard of New Fortunes* (1890) or Stephen Crane's *Sister Carrie* (1900), New York writers were by then in full pursuit of a gritty realism against which Janvier's amiable fictions seemed at best superficial. So, too, John Sloan and other painters of the Ashcan school had begun to see the urban landscape in a way that made Janvier's romantic sensibility appear stilted, old-fashioned, and naive; indeed, only months before his death, they helped stage the wildly controversial Armory Show, which gave Americans their first taste of modern artists like Vincent van Gogh and Marcel Duchamp. Just days before Janvier's death, moreover, a new generation of Greenwich Village radicals, led by John Reed of *The Masses* magazine, organized a landmark pageant in Madison Square Garden to raise money for striking textile workers in Paterson, New Jersey. And before the year was out, as if all that were not enough, F. W. Woolworth would complete his sixty-story "cathedral of commerce" on Broadway, a monument to the money-grubbing utilitarianism that Janvier blamed for the city's indifference to its past. Of all his books, only *In Old New York* has weathered that furious press of events, and with this new edition there is good reason to hope that it will continue to do so.

Edwin G. Burrows
Department of History
Brooklyn College

## SOURCES

Beard, Rick and Leslie Cohen Berlowitz, eds., *Greenwich Village: Culture and Counterculture*. New Brunswick: Rutgers University Press, 1993.

Burrows, Edwin G. and Mike Wallace, *Gotham: A History of New York City to 1898*. New York: Oxford University Press, 1999.

Exman, Eugene. *The House of Harper: One Hundred and Fifty Years of Publishing*. New York: Harper & Row, 1967.

Harper, J. Henry. *The House of Harper: A Century of Publishing in Franklin Square*. New York: Harper & Brothers, 1912.

Janvier, Thomas A. *At the Casa Napoleon*. Preface by Ripley Hitchcock. New York: Harper & Brothers, 1914.

Neeper, Layne. "Thomas Janvier," in *Nineteenth-Century American Fiction Writers*, edited by Kent P. Ljungquist. Detroit: Gale Research, 1999.

*New York Times*, June 19, 1913.

Rosenwaike, Ira. *Population History of New York City*. Syracuse: Syracuse University Press, 1972.

# IN OLD NEW YORK

# In Old New York

## THE EVOLUTION OF NEW YORK

### I

THERE was no element of permanence in the settlement of New York. The traders sent here under Hendrick Christiansen, immediately upon Hudson's return to Holland in 1609, had no intention of remaining in America beyond the time that would pass while their ships crossed the sea and came again for the furs which meanwhile they were to secure. Even when Fort Manhattan was erected—the stockade that was built about the year 1614 just south of the present Bowling Green—this structure was intended only for the temporary shelter of the factors of the United New Netherland Company while engaged with the Indians in transient trade; for the life of this trading organization specifically was limited by its charter to four voyages, all to be made within the three years beginning January 1, 1615. Fort Manhattan, therefore, simply was a trading-post. If the Company's charter could be renewed, the post would be continued while it was profitable; upon the expiration of the charter, or when the post ceased to be profitable, it would be abandoned. That the temporary settlement thus made might develop, later, into a permanent town was a matter wholly aside from the interests in view. Leavenworth, Denver, a dozen of our Western cities, have been founded in precisely the same fashion within our own day.

Not until the year 1621, when the Dutch West India Company came into existence, were considerate measures taken for assuring a substantial colonial life to the Dutch settlement in America. The earlier trading association, the United New Netherland Company, expired by limitation on the last day of the year 1617; but its privileges were revived and maintained by annual grant for at least two years; probably for three. Then the larger organization was formed, with chartered rights (so far as the power to grant these lay with the States General of Holland) to the exclusive trade of all the coasts of both Americas.

Unlike the English trading companies—whose administration of their colonial establishments flowed from a central source—the Dutch West India Company was in the nature of a commercial federation. Branches of the Company were established in the several cities of Holland; which branches, while subject to the authority (whereof they themselves were part) of the organization as a whole, enjoyed distinct rights and privileges: having assigned to them, severally, specific territories, over which they exercised the right of government, and with which they possessed the exclusive right to trade.

In accordance with this scheme of arrangement, the trading-post on the island of Manhattan, with its dependent territory—broadly claimed as extending along the coast from the Virginia Plantations northward to New England, and inland indefinitely—became the portion of the Amsterdam branch ; wherefore the name of New Amsterdam was given to the post, even as the territory already had received the name of New Netherland.

As a commercial undertaking, the Dutch West India Company was admirably organized. Its projectors sought to establish it on so substantial a foundation that its expansion would not be subject to sudden checks, but would proceed equably and steadily from the start. To meet these requirements, mere trading-posts in foreign countries were not sufficient. Such temporary establishments were liable to be effaced in a moment, either by resident savages or by visiting savages afloat out of Europe—for in that cheerful period of the world's history all was game that could be captured at large upon or on the borders of the ocean sea. For the security of the Company, therefore, it was necessary that the New Netherland should be held not by the loose tenure of a small fort lightly garrisoned, but by the strong tenure of a colonial establishment firmly rooted in the soil  With this accomplished, the attacks

of savages of any sort were not especially to be
dreaded. Colonists might be killed in very considerable numbers and still (the available supply
of colonists being ample) no great harm would be
done to the Company's interests, for the colony
would survive. Therefore it was that with the
change in ownership and in name came also a
change in the nature of the Dutch hold upon this
island. Fort Manhattan had been an isolated
settlement established solely for purposes of
trade ; New Amsterdam was the nucleus of a colonial establishment, and was the seat of a colonial government which nominally controlled a
region as large as all the European possessions of
Holland and the German states combined.

It would be absurd, however, to take very seriously this government that was established in the
year 1623. The portion of the American continent over which Director Minuit exercised absolutely undisputed authority was not quite the
whole of the territory (now enclosed by the lower loop of the elevated railway) which lies south
of the present Battery Place. Within that micro-
scopic principality he ruled ; outside of it he only
reigned. That he was engaged in the rather
magnificent work of founding what was to be the
chief city of the Continent was far too monstrous
a thought to blast its way to his imaginative
faculty through the thickness of his substantial
skull.

Yet Fort Amsterdam, begun about the year
1626 — its northern wall about on the line of

the existing row of houses facing the Bowling Green — really was the beginning of the present city. The engineer who planned it, Kryn Frederick, had in mind the creation of works sufficiently large to shelter in time of danger all the inhabitants of a considerable town; and, when the Fort was finished, the fact that such a stronghold existed was one of the inducements extended by the West India Company to secure its needed colonists: for these, being most immediately and personally interested in the matter, could not be expected to contemplate the possibility of their own massacre by savages of the land or sea in the same large and statesmanlike manner that such accidents of colonial administration were regarded by the Company's directors. The building of the Fort, therefore, was the first step towards anchoring the colony firmly to the soil. By the time that the Fort was finished the population of this island amounted to about two hundred souls; and the island itself, for a consideration of $24, had been bought by Director Minuit for the Company: and so formally had passed to Dutch from Indian hands.

While the town of New Amsterdam thus came into existence under the protection of the guns of its Fort, the back country also was filling up rapidly with settlers. In the year 1629 the decree issued that any member of the West India Company who, under certain easy conditions, should form a settlement of not less than fifty persons, none of whom should be under fifteen years of age, should be granted a tract of land fronting sixteen miles upon the sea, or upon any navigable river (or eight miles when both shores of the river were occupied), and extending thence inland indefinitely; and that the *patroons* to whom such grants of land should be made should exercise manorial rights over their estates. In accordance with the liberal provisions of this decree, settlements quickly were made on both sides of the Hudson and on the lands about the bay; but these settlements were founded in strict submission to the capital; and by the grant to the latter (by the Charter of Liberties and Exemptions, 1629) of staple rights—the obligation laid upon all vessels trading in the rivers or upon the coast to discharge cargo at the Fort, or, in lieu thereof, to pay compensating port charges—the absolute commercial supremacy of the capital was assured. Thus, almost contemporaneously with its founding, the town of New Amsterdam—at once the seat of government and the centre of trade—became in a very small way what later it was destined to be in a very large way : a metropolis.


II


The tangle of crowded streets below the Bowling Green testifies even to the present day to the haphazard fashion in which the foundations of this city were laid.   Each settler, apparently, was free to put his house where he pleased ; and to surround it by an enclosure of any shape and, within reason, of any size. Later, streets were opened—for the most part by promoting existing foot-paths and lanes—along the confines of these arbitrarily ordered parcels of land. In this random fashion grew up the town.

Excepting Philadelphia, all of our cities on the Atlantic seaboard have started in the same careless way: in as marked contrast with the invariably orderly pre-arrangement of the cities in the lands to the south of us as is the contrast between the Saxon and the Latin minds. Yet the piece-made city has to commend it a lively personality to which the whole-made city never attains. The very defects in its putting together give it the charm of individuality; breathe into it with a subtle romance (that to certain natures is most strongly appealing) somewhat of the very essence of the long-by dead to whom its happy unreasonableness is due; preserve to it tangibly the tradition of the burning moment when the metal, now hardened, came fluent from the crucible and the casting of the city was begun.

Actually, only two roads were established when the town of New Amsterdam was founded, and these so obviously were necessary that, practically, they established themselves. One of them, on the line of the present Stone and Pearl streets—the latter then the water-front—led from the Fort to the Brooklyn ferry at about the present Peck Slip. The other, on the line of the present Broadway, led northward from the Fort, past farms and gar-

dens falling away toward the North River, as far
as the present Park Row; and along the line of
that street, and of Chatham Street, and of the
Bowery, went on into the wilderness. After the
palisade was erected, this road was known as far
as the city gate (at Wall Street) as the Heere
Straat, or High Street; and beyond the wall as
the Heere Wegh — for more than a century, the
only highway that traversed the island from end
to end.

Broad Street and the Beaver's Path primarily
were not streets at all. On the line of the first
of these, with a roadway on each side, a canal extended as far as Beaver Street; where it narrowed
to a ditch which drained the swamp that extended
northward to about the present Exchange Place.
On the line of the Beaver's Path, east and west
from the main ditch, were lateral ditches at the
lower end of the swamp. This system of surface drainage having converted the swamp into a
meadow, it became known as the Sheep Pasture.
That the primitive conditions have not been wholly changed was made manifest within the past
three years by the very extensive system of piling
which was the necessary preparation to the erection of the ten-story building on the northwest
corner of Broad and Beaver streets. Down beneath the modern surface the ancient swamp remains to this present day.

Because of the homelikeness—as one sat contentedly smoking on one's stoop in the cool of
summer evenings — that there was in having a

ALONG THE CANAL IN OLD MANHATTAN

good strong-smelling canal under one's nose, and pleasant sight of round squat sailor-men aboard of boats which also were of a squat roundness, Broad Street (then called the Heere Graft) was a favorite dwelling-place with the quality of that early day; and even the Beaver's Path — which could boast only a minor, ditchlike smell, that yet was fit to bring tears of homesickness into one's eyes, such tender associations did it arouse—was well thought of by folk of the humbler sort, to whom the smell of a whole canal was too great a luxury.

Finally, one other street came into existence in that early time as the outgrowth of constraining conditions; this was the present Wall Street, which primitively was the open way, known as the Cingle, in the rear of the city wall. As to the wall, it was built under stress of danger and amidst great excitement. When the news came, March 13, 1653, of a threatened foray hither of New-Englanders—a lithe, slippery, aggressive race, for which every right-thinking Dutchman entertained a vast contempt, wherein also was a dash of fear— there was a prodigious commotion in this city: of which the immediate and most wonderful manifestation was a session of the General Council so charged with vehement purpose that it continued all day long! In the morning the Council resolved "that the whole body of citizens shall keep watch by night, in such places as shall be designated, the City Tavern to be the temporary headquarters; that the Fort shall be repaired; that

some way must be devised to raise money; that
Captain Vischer shall be requested to fix his sails,
to have his piece loaded, and to keep his vessel
in readiness; that, because the Fort is not large
enough to contain all the inhabitants, it is deemed
necessary to enclose the city with breast-works
and palisades." And then, in the afternoon of
this same momentous day—after strenuously dining—the Council prepared a list for a forced levy
by which the sum of five thousand guilders was to
be raised for purposes of defence. Having thus
breathlessly discharged itself of so tremendous a
rush of business, it is not surprising that the Council held no sitting on the ensuing day, but de-
voted itself solely to recuperative rest; nor that
it suffered a whole week to elapse before it prepared specifications for the palisades—the erection of which thereafter proceeded at a temperate
speed.

Fortunately for themselves, the New-Englanders stayed at home. Governor Stuyvesant, being
a statesman of parts, doubtless saw to it that news
was conveyed across the Connecticut of the land-
sturm which arose in its might each night and
made its headquarters at the City Tavern—whence
it was ready to rush forth, armed with curiously
shaped Dutch black bottles, to pour a devastating
fire of hot schnapps upon the foe. Wherefore the
New-Englanders, being filled with a wholesome
dread of such a valorous company — well in its
cups, and otherwise fuming with patriotic rage—
wisely elected to give this city a wide berth; and

it is but just to add that Dominie Megapolensis claimed some share in averting the threatened direful conflict because at his instigation Governor Stuyvesant, in view of the unhappy state of affairs, appointed the ninth day of April, 1653, as a day of general fasting and prayer.

As the wall never was needed, its erection actually did more harm than good. For nearly half a century its effect was to restrain that natural expansion northward of the city which certainly would have begun earlier had it not been for the presence of this unnecessary barrier. Yet even without the wall there would have been no such quick development of the suburbs as characterizes the growth of cities in these modern times. The fact must be remembered that for a century after the wall was built—that is, until long after it was demolished — the inherited tendency to pack houses closely together still was overwhelmingly strong. For centuries and centuries every European city, even every small town, had been cramped within stone corsets until the desire for free breathing almost was lost. Long after the necessity for it had vanished the habit of constriction remained.

Excepting these five streets—Pearl (including Stone), Broadway, Broad, Beaver, and Wall; to which, perhaps, Whitehall should be added, because that thoroughfare originally was the open way left on the land side of the Fort—all of the old streets in the lower part of the city are the outcome of individual need or whim. The new

streets in this region—South, Front, part of Water, Greenwich, Washington, and West—are the
considerate creations of later times, all of them
having been won from the water by filling in beyond the primitive line of high tide.

Having thus contrived—by the simple process
of permitting every man to make lanes and
streets according to the dictates of his own fancy
—to lay out as pretty a little tangle of a town as
could be found just then in all Christendom, and
a town which resembled in the crooks of its
crookedness (to an extent that was altogether
heart-moving) the intricate region just eastward
of the Botermarkt in the ancient city after which
it was named, the Governor in Council, about the
year 1653, promulgated a decree that a map
should be made of New Amsterdam : and that
the town should remain from that time forward
without alteration.

Doubtless Jacques Cortelyou, the official surveyor, executed the first part of this decree ; but
very diligent search in this country and in Holland has failed as yet to bring to light the map
which he then made. The most widely known
early map, therefore, is " The Duke's Plan " (as it
usually is styled), which represents " the town of
Mannados or New Amsterdam as it was in September, 1661," being a draft made in the year
1664, upon the capture of the town by the English, to be sent to the Duke of York. Presumably, this map differs from Cortelyou's map only
in showing a few more houses, in the substitution

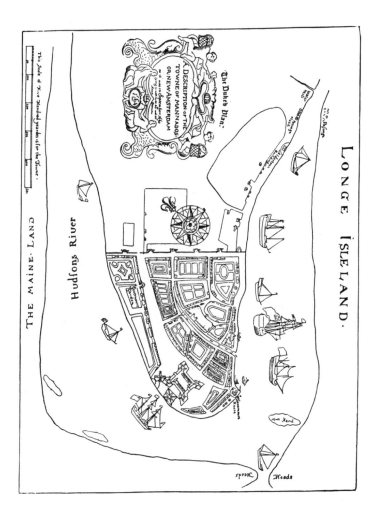

The Dutch Plan.

A DESCRIPTION of THE
TOWNE of MANNADOS
OR NEW-AMSTERDAM
as it was in September 1661

LONGE ISLELAND.

THE MAINE·LAND

Hudsons River

This Scale of Five Hundred yeardes is for the Towne.

of English for Dutch text, and in its gallant display of the English flag.*

The Duke's Plan is of exceeding interest, in that it exhibits the extent of the town at the moment when it passed from Dutch to English ownership: a triangle whereof the base was the present Wall Street, and the sides were on the lines of the present Water, Front, State, and Greenwich streets, which then, approximately, were the lines of high tide. Nor was even this small area closely built up — by far the larger part of it being given over to garden plots in which fair Dutch cabbages grew. The northern limit of the map is about the present Roosevelt Street, where Old Wreck Brook (as it was called later) discharged the waters of the Fresh Water pond into the East River across the region which still is known as "The Swamp." All told, there were but twelve buildings outside of the wall: of which the most important were the storehouses belonging to Isaac Allerton close by the "passageway" to Brooklyn—that is to say, the present Peck Slip. Inside the wall the only block built up solidly was that between Bridge and Stone streets — then divided by the Winckel

---

* The earliest map of New York known to be in existence is that now in the possession of Mr. Henry Harisse: a plan of "Manatus, drawn on the spot by Joan Vingboons in 1639"; to which great additional value is given by its marginal legend recording the names of the first forty-five householders on this island. This most precious document was exhibited in July, 1892, in Paris at the Columbian exhibition of maps and globes

ON THE RIVER FRONT

Straat, upon which stood the five stone store-houses of the Dutch West India Company. This was the business centre of the town, because here were the landing-places. From the foot of Moor Street (which may have derived its name, now corrupted to Moore, from the fact that it was the mooring-place), the single wharf within the town limits extended out a little beyond the line of the present Water Street. Here, and also upon the banks of the canal in the present Broad Street, lighters discharged and received the cargoes of ships lying in the stream. Already, as is shown by the houses dotted along the East River front outside the wall, the tendency of the town was to grow towards the northeast ; and this was natural, for the Perel Straat—leading along the water-side to the Brooklyn ferry—was the most travelled thoroughfare in the town.

In the year 1661, when the draft was made from which The Duke's Plan was copied, New Amsterdam was a town of about one thousand souls, under the government, organized in 1652, of a schout, two burgomasters, and five schepens. The western side of the town, from the Bowling Green northward, was a gentle wilderness of or-chards and gardens and green fields. On the eastern side the farthest outlying dwelling was Wolfert Webber's tavern, on the northern high-way near the present Chatham Square—whereat travellers adventuring into the northern wilds of this island were wont to pause for a season while they put up a prayer or two for protection, and

at the same time made their works conform to
their faith by taking aboard a sufficient store of
Dutch courage to carry them pot - valiantly onward until safe harbor was made again within the
Harlem tavern's friendly walls.  Save for the Indian settlement at Sappokanican (near the present
Gansevoort Market) and the few farm-houses scattered along the highway, all this region was desert
of human life.  Annual round-ups were held, under
the supervision of the Brand-master, of the herds
which ran wild in the bush country whereof the beginning was about where the City Hall now stands.

And upon the town rested continually the
dread of Indian assault.  At any moment the
hot - headed act of some angry colonist might
easily bring on a war.  In the early autumn of
1655, when peaches were ripe, an assault actually
was made: being a vengeance against the whites
because Hendrick Van Dyke had shot to death
an Indian woman whom he found stealing peaches in his orchard (lying just south of the present
Rector Street) on the North River shore.  Fortunately, warning came to the townsfolk, and,
crowding their women and children into the Fort,
they were able to beat off the savages; whereupon the savages, being the more eager for re-
venge, fell upon the settlements about Pavonia
and on Staten Island: where the price paid for
Hendrick Van Dyke's peaches was the wasting
of twenty-eight farms, the bearing away of one
hundred and fifty Christians into captivity, and
one hundred Christians outright slain.

## III

At eight o'clock on the morning of September 8, 1664, the flag of the Dutch West India Company fell from Fort Amsterdam, and the flag of England went up over what then became Fort James. Governor Stuyvesant—even his wooden leg sharing in his air of dejection—marched dismally his conquered forces out from the main gateway, across the Parade to the Beaver's Path, and so to the Heere Graft, where boats were lying to carry them to the ships at anchor in the stream. And at the same time the English marched gallantly down Broadway—from where they had been waiting, about in front of where Aldrich Court now stands—and Governor Nicolls solemnly took possession of New Amsterdam, and of all the New Netherland, in the name of the English sovereign, and for the use of the Duke of York.

This change of ownership, with which came also a change of name, was largely and immediately beneficial to the colony. Under the government of the Dutch West India Company, the New Netherland had been managed not as a national dependency, but as a commercial venture which was expected to bring in a handsome return. Much more than the revenue necessary to maintain a government was required of the colonists; and at the same time the restrictions im-

THE SURRENDER OF FORT AMSTERDAM

posed upon private trade—to the end that the
trade of the Company might be increased—were
so onerous as materially to diminish the earning
power of the individual, and so correspondingly
to make the burden of taxation the heavier to
bear.   Nor could there be between the colonists
and the Company—as there could have been between the colonists and even a severe home government—a tie of loyalty.   Indeed, the situation
had become so strained under this commercial
despotism that the inhabitants of New Amsterdam almost openly sided with the English when

the formal demand for surrender was made, and the town passed into British possession and became New York without the striking of a single blow.

Virtually, this was the end of Dutch ownership hereabouts. Once again, from July 30, 1673, until November 10, 1674, the Dutch were in possession—following that "clap of thunder on a fair frosty day," as Sir William Temple called it, when England declared war against Holland in the year 1672. But this temporary reclamation had no influence beyond slightly retarding the great development of the city, and of all the colony, which came with English rule.

Although the New Netherland had been acquired, nominally, by force of arms, New York by no means was treated as a conquered province. Colonel Richard Nicolls, who commanded the English military force, and who became the first English Governor of the Province, conducted his government with such wise conservatism that there was no shock whatever in the transition from the old to the new order of things, and the change was most apparent in agreeable ways. Not until three-fourths of a year had passed was the city government re-organized, in accordance with English customs, by substituting for the schout, burgomasters, and schepens, a sheriff, board of aldermen, and a mayor; and even when the change was made it was apparent rather than real, for most of the old officers simply continued to carry on the government under new names.

The Governor's Commission, of June 12, 1665, by
which this change was effected, is known as the
Nicolls Charter. It did actually slightly enlarge
the authority of the municipal government; but
its chief importance was its demonstration of the
intention of the English to treat New York not
as a commercial investment, but as a colonial
capital entitled to consideration and respect.

The most emphatic and the most far-reachingly
beneficial expression of this fostering policy was
the passage, in the year 1678, of what was styled
the Bolting Act; in accordance with the provisions of which this city was granted a monopoly in the bolting of flour, and in the packing of
flour and biscuit for export under the act. No
mill outside of the city was permitted to grind
flour for market, nor was any person outside of
the city permitted to pack breadstuffs in any
form for sale; the result of which interdict was
to throw the export trade in breadstuffs, mainly
with the West Indies and already very considerable, exclusively into the hands of the millers and
merchants of New York. Outside of the city,
and with justice, this law was regarded with ex-
treme disfavor. From the first, strong efforts
were made by the country people to secure its
repeal; but the "pull" of the city members in
the Provincial Assembly (the whole matter has
an interestingly prophetic flavor), was strong
enough to keep it in effect for sixteen years. At
last, in 1694, the country members broke away
from their city leaders (as has happened also in

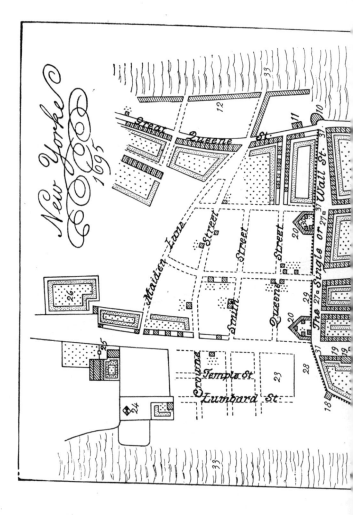

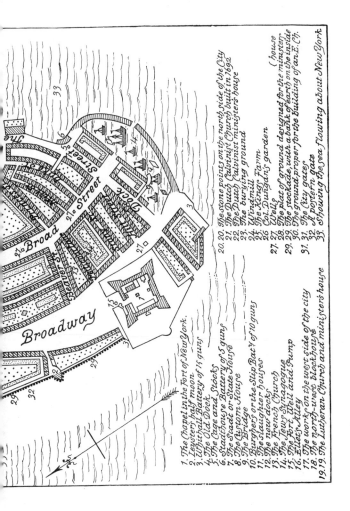

1. The Chapel in the Fort of New York.
2. Leyster's half moon.
3. Whitehall Battery of 15 guns.
4. The Old Dock.
5. The Cage and Stocks.
6. Stadthouse Battery of 5 guns.
7. The Stadt or State House.
8. The Custom House.
9. The Bridge.
10. Burghers or the Slip Bat'y of 10 guns.
11. The Slaughter houses.
12. The new dock.
13. The French Church.
14. The Jews Synagogue.
15. The Fort Well and Pump.
16. Ellery Alley.
17. The works on the west side of the city.
18. The north-west block-house.
19.19. The Lutheran Church and minister's house.
20.20. The stone points on the north side of the City.
21. The Dutch Calvinist Church built in 1692.
22. The Dutch Calvinist minister's house.
23. The burying ground.
24. Windmill.
25. The King's Farm.
26. Col. Dungan's garden.
27.27. Wells.
28. The plot of ground designed for the minister's house.
29.29. The stockade, with a bank of earth on the inside.
30. The ground proper for the building of an E. Ch.
31.31. The City gate.
32. A postern gate.
33. Showing the sea flowing about New York.

later times) and most righteously repealed this very one-sided law.

But the Bolting Act had been in force long enough to accomplish a result larger and more lasting than its promoters had contemplated, or, indeed, than they well could comprehend : it had laid the foundation of the foreign commerce of New York.

During the sixteen years that the act remained operative the city expanded, under the stimulus of such extraordinary privileges, by leaps and bounds. Fortunately, an authoritative record has been preserved — in the petition filed by the New York millers and merchants against the repeal of the act—of precisely what the city gained in this short space of time.    In the year 1678 (the petitioners state), the total number of houses in New York was 384 ; the total number of beef cattle slaughtered was 400 ; the sailing craft hailing from the port consisted of three ships, seven boats, and eight sloops; and the total annual revenues of the city were less than £2000.    On the other hand, in the year 1694 the number of houses had increased to 983 ; the slaughter of beef cattle (largely for export), to nearly 4000 ; the sailing craft to 60 ships, 40 boats, and 25 sloops; and the city revenues to £5000.    In conclusion, to show how intimately this prodigious expansion was associated with the milling interest, the petitioners declared that more than 600 of the 983 buildings in the city depended in one way or another upon the trade in flour.    In view of these facts, very properly do the arms of New York—granted in the year 1682, in the midst of its first burst of great prosperity—exhibit, along with the beaver emblematic of the city's commercial beginning, the sails of a windmill and two flour-barrels as emblems of the firm foundation upon which its foreign commerce has been reared.

By comparing the map of 1695 with the Duke's Plan of 1664 the development of the city under the influence of the Bolting Act may be seen at a glance. In 1664 fully one-third of the available street-front space remained vacant in the city proper, and only eighteen buildings had been erected outside of the wall. By 1695 the six hundred new buildings had occupied almost all the available street-front space in the city proper, and had forced the laying out of so large a group of new streets to the northward of the wall that the city had been almost doubled in size. In the annexed district few houses had been erected west of King (William) Street; and the new streets west of Broadway possibly had not even been opened — for the growth of the town still was toward the northeast. But the many new buildings east of King Street, and the provision upon so large a scale of new streets, showed the alert enterprising spirit that was abroad. This was, indeed, the most active period in real-estate transactions that the city so far had known. Prices were rising prodigiously. By the year 1689 fourteen lots near Coenties Slip were sold at auction for £35 each, and a lot at the foot of Broad Street actually was valued at £80. However, while affected by the rise in real-estate values generally, the extraordinary rise in prices hereabouts was due to the building at the foot of Broad Street — at the same time that the canal was filled in—of the Wet Docks: two basins of a sufficient size to harbor a whole fleet of the little ships of that day while their cargoes were taken in or discharged. And about the same time, so rapidly was the commerce of the city increasing, two new wharves were built upon the East River front. Finally, in the midst of this most flourishing period, New York received, April 22, 1686, the very liberal charter—known as the Dongan Charter, because granted through the Governor of that name—which still is the basis of our civic rights.*

During this energetic and highly formative period, while wise and sound English government was doing so much to foster the welfare of the city, the English race distinctly was in a minority among the citizens. This fact is brought out clearly in the following statement made by Governor Dongan, in the year 1687, in his report to the Board of Trade: " For the past seven years

* The Dongan Charter, granted by James II., was amended by Queen Anne in 1708, and was farther enlarged by George II. in 1730 into what is known as the Montgomery Charter. This last, confirmed by the General Assembly of the Province in 1732, made New York virtually a free city. The Mayor was appointed by the Governor in Council until the Revolution, by the State Governor and four members of the Council of Appointment until 1821, by the Common Council of the city until 1834, and since this last date (in theory) by the people.

there have not come over to this Province twenty English, Scotch, or Irish families. On Long Island the people increase so fast that they complain for want of land, and many remove thence to the neighboring provinces. Several French families have lately come from the West Indies and from England, and also several Dutch families from Holland, so that the number of foreigners greatly exceeds the King's natural born subjects."

In point of morals, the New York of two hundred years ago seems to have been about on a par with frontier towns and outpost settlements of the present day. About the time that Governor Dongan made his report to the Board of Trade, the Rev. John Miller—for three years a resident of the colony as chaplain to the King's forces—addressed to the then Bishop of London a letter in which he reviewed the spiritual shortcomings of the colonists. Mr. Miller's strictures upon the Dissenters, naturally warped by his point of view, scarcely are to be quoted in fairness; but of the clergymen of the Establishment, toward whom his disposition would be lenient, he thus wrote: "There are here, and also in other provinces, many of them such as, being of a vicious life and conversation, have played so many vile pranks, and show such an ill light, as have been very prejudicial to religion in general and to the Church of England in particular." Continuing, he complains broadly of "the great negligence of divine things that is generally found in the peo-

THE WET DOCKS, FOOT OF BROAD STREET

pie, of what sect or sort soever they pretend to be." And, in conclusion, he declares: "In a soil so rank as this no marvel if the Evil One finds a ready entertainment for the seed he is ready to cast in; and from a people so inconstant and regardless of heaven and holy things no wonder if God withdraw His grace, and give them up a prey to those temptations which they so industriously seek to embrace."

These cheering remarks relate to the Province at large. Touching the citizens of New York in particular, the reverend gentleman briefly but forcibly describes them as drunkards and gamblers, and adds: "This, joined to their profane, atheistical, and scoffing method of discourse, makes their company extremely uneasy to sober and religious men."

## IV

On the turn from the seventeenth to the eighteenth century, the population of New York was about 5000 souls: Dutch and English nearly equal in numbers; a few French, Swedes, and Jews; about 800 negroes, nearly all of whom were slaves. It was a driving, prosperous, commercial community; nor is there much cause for wonder—in view of the Rev. Mr. Miller's pointed lament over its ungodliness — that a great deal of its prosperity came through channels which now would be regarded as intolerably foul. But in those brave days natures were strong, and squeamish-

ness was a weakling virtue still hidden in the
womb of time.

Slave-dealing then was an important and well-
thought-of industry — or, in the more elegant
phrase of one of the gravest of New York historians, " a species of maritime adventure then engaged in by several of our most respectable merchants." The Dutch are credited with having
brought the first cargo of slaves to the northern
part of America—from their possessions on the
Guinea Coast to the Virginia plantations—and a
regular part of the business of the Dutch West
India Company was providing African slaves for
use in its American colonies. The profits of the
business—even allowing for the bad luck of a high
death-rate on the western passage—were so allur-
ingly great that it was not one to be slighted by
the eminently go-ahead merchants of this town;
and the fact must be remembered that, as a business, slave-dealing was quite as legitimate then as
is the emigrant traffic of the present day. Young
Mr. John Cruger has left on record a most edifying account of a voyage which he made out of New
York in the years 1698–1700, in the ship *Prophet
Daniel*, to Madagascar for the purchase of live
freight; and the sentiment of the community in
the premises is exhibited by the fact that the
slave-dealing Mr. Cruger was elected an alderman
from the Dock Ward continuously from the year
1712 until the year 1733, and that subsequently
he served four consecutive terms as mayor. In
addition to the negro slaves, there were many Ind-

ian slaves held in the colony. For convenience in hiring, the law was passed, November 30, 1711, that "all negro and Indian slaves that are let out to hire within the city do take up their standing in order to be hired at the market-house at the Wall Street Slip."

Probably the alarm bred of the so-called Negro Plot of 1741 was most effective in checking the growth of slavery in this city. Certainly, the manner in which the negroes charged with fomenting this problematical conspiracy were dealt with affords food for curious reflection upon the social conditions of the times. After a trial that would have been a farce had it not been a tragedy, Clause was condemned to be "broke upon a wheel"; Robin to be hung in chains alive, "and so to continue without any sustenance until he be dead"; Tom to be "burned with a slow fire until he be dead and consumed to ashes," and so on. However, everything depends upon the point of view. In that strong-stomached time judicial cruelty to criminals met with universal approval; and as to slavery, the worshipful Sir Edward Coke, but a very few years earlier, had laid down the doctrine that pagans properly could be held in bondage by Christians, because the former were the bond-slaves of Satan, while the latter were the servants of God.

When it came to piracy, public opinion in New York was not keyed up to a pitch that could be called severe; and it is a fact that the foundations of some highly respectable fortunes still ex-

tant in this community were laid in successful
ventures — to use the euphuistic phrase of the
day—" on the account." Under the generously
liberal rule of Governor Fletcher (1692–8), any
pirate, or any New York merchant taking what a
Wall Street man of the present day would term
"a flyer" in piracy, was entirely secure in his
business provided he was willing to pay a fair
percentage of its profits to that high functionary
(even as the modern city contractor is secure if he
will "stand in" with the right city officials); because of which cordial leniency matters here became such a hissing and reproach that the home
government was compelled to recall Fletcher and
to send out in his place Lord Bellomont—who
specifically was charged with the duty of break-
ing up what elegantly was styled "the Red Sea
trade."

Much of this piracy was carried on under
cover of privateering ; and from genuine privateering — which was held to be an entirely
honest and legitimate business—the city derived
a large amount of wealth. During almost the
whole of the century of nearly continuous warfare that began in the year 1689, with the accession of William of Orange to the English throne,
there were fine chances for private armed ventures against England's enemies on the high seas.
From this port, most notably in the first and
fourth decades of the last century, a dashing fleet
of privateers went forth; and *The Weekly Post Boy*
of the later period blazes with calls "to all Gentle-

men Sailors, and others, who have a mind to try their Fortunes on a Cruizing Voyage against the enemy," to enter on one or another of the private armed vessels about to put to sea. In addition to the many prizes taken by the privateers, many prizes taken by King's ships—about this time the dashing Captain Warren commanded on this station—were sent into New York to be condemned; and it is not impossible that these last netted almost as much to the ingenuous merchants who had the handling of them as did the out-and-out captures on private account.

And all the while that money thus easily was coming in over the bar at Sandy Hook with almost every tide, substantial business interests of a quieter sort, yet in the long-run more solidly profitable, were in the course of development. Especially did the West India trade—so firmly established by the Bolting Act that the repeal of that act did not do it any lasting injury—become constantly of increasing importance. It did not, of course, bring in the great profits which came from it while the city held the monopoly of milling; but it was conducted so intelligently—provisions shipped hence being exchanged for West Indian products; these in turn being shipped to England and exchanged for manufactured goods and wares; and these last being brought to this city for sale or trade—that each round of transactions left three profits in the merchants' hands. At the same time a considerable coastwise trade was maintained; and a large business was done in

ship-building—ships even being built in this city
to be sent to England for sale.

According to figures preserved in the chance
letter of a German traveller, Professor Kalm, 211
vessels entered and 222 vessels cleared from this
port between December 1, 1729, and December 5,
1730. By the year 1732 the population of the
city had increased to 8624 souls; and in this same
year the advance in the value of real estate was
made manifest by the sale of seven lots on Whitehall Street at prices varying from £150 to £200.

The extent of New York at the end of the
first quarter of the eighteenth century is shown
by the map drawn by James Lyne from a survey
made in the year 1729; and the fact which this
map most strongly emphasizes is the continued
growth of the city northeastward and the continued unimportance of Broadway. At that period several causes were united to discourage the
development of the western side of the island
and to encourage the development of the eastern
side: as has been the case again in our own
times, when we have seen the most desirable
part of New York—the Riverside region north
of Seventy-second Street—suddenly spring into
popular favor after years of entire neglect. At
the beginning of the last century practically all
the business interests of the city were centred
on or near the East River front. Here, from the
docks at Whitehall Street northward to Roosevelt's wharf, all the shipping of the port was har-
bored — for the practical reason that the salt

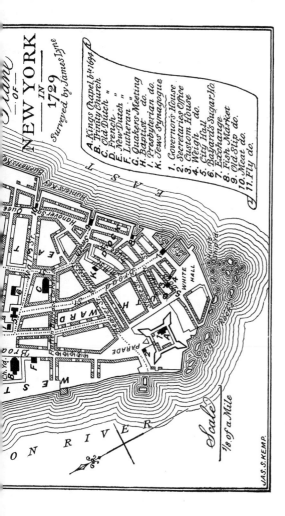

Plan
— OF —
NEW YORK
IN
1729
Surveyed by James Lyne

A. Kings Chapel, b.t 1694
B. Trinity Church
C. Old Dutch  "
D. French  "
E. New Dutch  "
F. Lutheran  "
G. Quakers Meeting
H. Baptist  do.
I. Presbyterian do.
K. Jews Synagogue

1. Governors House
2. Secretaries Office
3. Custom House
4. Weigh  do.
5. City Hall  do.
6. Bayards Sugar Ho.
7. Exchange
8. Fish Market
9. Old Slip do.
10. Meat  do.
11. Fly  do.

Scale
⅛ of a Mile

JAS. S. KEMP.

water did not freeze, and that consequently the
shipping was safe in winter from ice; here, for
the same reason, were the yards of the ship-builders; here were the warehouses of the merchants;
and here, along Great Queen (Pearl) Street—the
street leading to the Brooklyn ferry—all the considerable shops were situated in order to make
sure of catching the Long Island trade.

Broadway actually was in a remote and obscure part of the town.   Below Crown (Liberty)
Street dwelling - houses had been erected, of
which a few near the Bowling Green were prodigiously fine; but north of Crown Street all the
west side of Broadway was open fields.   This unimproved region, beginning at the present Fulton
Street and thence extending northward, was the
Church Farm.*

The farm-house pertaining to this farm—standing very nearly upon the site of the present Astor

* The estate known as the Company's Farm, set aside by the
Dutch to be tilled for the benefit of the Company's servants,
civil and military, lay between the present Fulton and Warren
streets and Broadway and the North River.   Upon the English
conquest, this estate became the private property of the Duke of
York.   Subsequently, in the year 1670, by purchase from heirs
of Annetje Jans, the boundary of the Duke's Farm was carried
northward as far as the present Charlton Street; possibly as far as
the present Christopher Street.   When the Duke of York ascended
the throne the property became known as the King's Farm; and
as the Queen's Farm upon the accession of Queen Anne.   In this
last reign, in the year 1705, reserving a quit-rent of three shillings
(which was extinguished in 1786 by a payment in gross), the then
Governor, Lord Cornbury, granted the entire estate to the English
Church on the Island of New York.

House—is shown on Lyne's map, immediately to
the south of the Broadway rope-walk. Later it
became a tavern of some celebrity—the Drovers'
Inn, kept by Adam Vanderberg. Undoubtedly,
the church ownership of this large parcel of land
tended to delay its utilization for building purposes, and so helped to retard the extension of
the city on the line of Broadway. Even in those
early days the strongly American desire to build
on land owned in fee operated against the use of
leasehold property. Not until the need for the

T O  B E  S O L D,
AT Vendue, on Tuefday the 12th inft,
at the Houfe of Mr John Williams,
near Mr Lifpenard's : A Leafe from Trinity Church, for Old John's Land, for 12
Years to come. 9 · · · · · · · · ~

ADVERTISEMENT, 1766

Church Farm became pressing was it taken for
improvement on the only terms upon which it
could be acquired.

Maerschalck's map (1755) shows that by the
middle of the last century the growth of the city,
creating this pressing need, had warranted the
laying out of streets through the southern portion of the Church property, and that five-and-
twenty buildings had been erected between the
present Liberty Street and the palisade. But the
stronger tendency of growth, it will be observed,

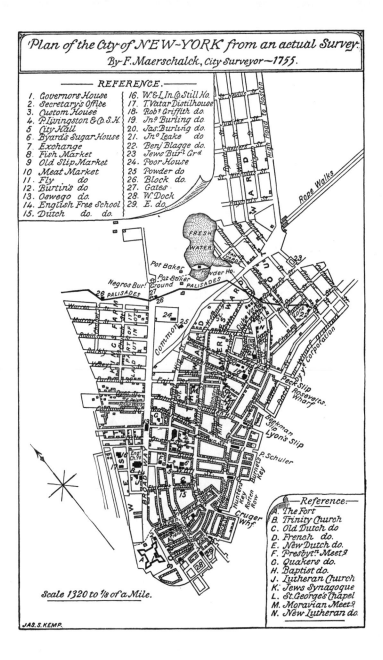

Plan of the City of NEW-YORK from an actual Survey.
By F. Maerschalck, City Surveyor—1755.

— REFERENCE. —

1. Governors House
2. Secretary's Office
3. Custom House
4. P. Livingston & O.S.H.
5. City Hall
6. Byard's Sugar House
7. Exchange
8. Fish Market
9. Old Slip Market
10. Meat Market
11. Fly      do
12. Burtin's do
13. Oswego  do.
14. English Free School
15. Dutch   do. do.

16. W. & L. In. Ca Still Ho.
17. T. Vatar Distilhouse
18. Robt Griffith do.
19. Jno Burling do.
20. Jas. Burling do.
21. Jno Leake  do
22. Benj Blagge do
23. Jews Burl Grd
24. Poor House
25. Powder do
26. Block.  do.
27. Gates
28. W. Dock
29. E.  do.

Rope Walks

FRESH WATER

Pot Baker
Pat Stiker
wder Ho.
PALISADES

Negros Bur! Ground

PALISADES

Common

Peck Slip
Rosevelts. Wharf
Beekman Slip
Lyon's Slip
P. Schuler

Hunters Key
Rotten Row
Burnet's Key

Cruger Whf.

— Reference: —

A.  The Fort
B.  Trinity Church
C.  Old Dutch do
D.  French   do.
E.  New Dutch do.
F.  Presbytn Meets
G.  Quakers do.
H.  Baptist do.
J.  Lutheran Church
K.  Jews Synagogue
L.  St. George's Chapel
M.  Moravian Meets
N.  New Lutheran do.

Scale 1320 to ⅛ of a Mile.

JAS. S. KEMP.

still was toward the northeast. This was, in
fact, the line of least resistance. Advance up the
middle of the island was blocked by the Fresh
Water pond, and up the western side it was im-
peded by the marshy valley known as Lispenard's Meadows; through the midst of which, on
the line of the present Canal Street, was the artificial drain from the Fresh Water to the North
River. Before this low-lying region was reached,
the obstacle caused by the leaseholds was encountered. Finally, the base-line of west-side
development, an extension of Broadway, was but
a lane leading to cow pastures and stopping
frankly, not far from the present Leonard Street,
at a set of bars. Not until the road, now Greenwich Street, leading to Greenwich Village was
opened (at an uncertain date, anterior to 1760)
was there any thoroughfare on the western side
of the island. The only life in this isolated suburb, therefore, was that of its few inhabitants:
who dwelt here for economy's sake, far removed
from the agreeable activities of the town.

On the eastern side of the island all was energy
and go. Here were centred all the important
business interests, and the base-line for farther
development was the Boston Post Road—a blithe
and bustling highway, along which ebbed and
flowed constantly a strong tide of travel between
the city and its dependent villages and the populous region lying inland from Long Island Sound.
Upon this highway—called in its lower reaches
the Bowery Lane, because of the farms or *bouer-*

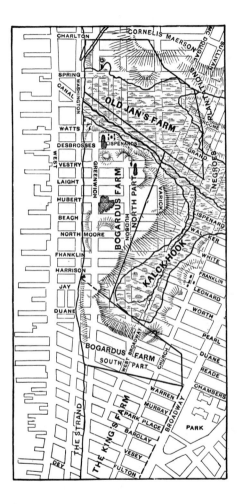

*ies* thereabouts—settlements had been made very early in colonial times; and by the third quarter of the eighteenth century—as is shown on Ratzen's larger map (1767)— there was an almost continuous line of country-seats extending as far northward as the present Madison Square. At the intersection of the highway with Monument Lane (of which lane two sections survive, in the present Astor Place and Greenwich Avenue) was the nucleus of a village; and Greenwich, to which the lane led, was a village of some importance. In a word, the growth of the city on this line was inevitable; for here, to the thrust of the expanding community was added the attraction of the settlements already established beyond the city's bounds.

On the smaller of Ratzen's maps, also of 1767, the great extension of the city in the twelve years following 1755 is strikingly exhibited; but the scheme of drafting—showing projected streets as though they actually were in existence, and not showing individual houses—is such that no precise concept can be formed of the actual gain. Most of this map is mere prophecy, of which the fulfilment did not come for more than a score and a half of years; and the very best of its prophecies, the Great Square, never was fulfilled at all. This liberal project for establishing a public park on the line of Grand Street — in a part of the city now most urgently in need of precisely such a breathing-space—had its origin in a speculative desire to provide an agreeable

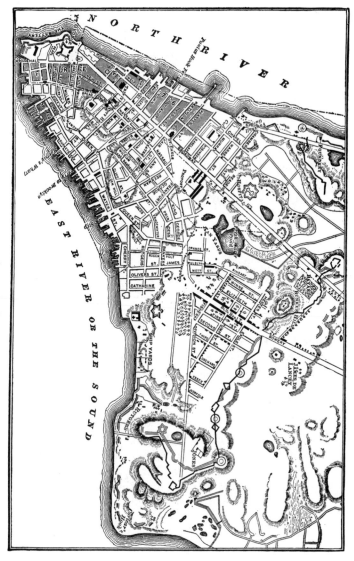

spot for suburban homes. That it was alive nine
years later is shown by the fact that the square—
then called De Lancey Square—appears on Major Holland's map, drawn from surveys made in
1776. But that was the last of it. On Hills s
map, 1782, close upon the present line of Grand
Street, the British earth-works grimly traverse
the very place where the park should be. In
common with every other phase or promise of
the city's prosperity, the Great Square was
ploughed under by the Revolutionary war.

V

New York suffered greater hardships during
the fight for Independence than fell to the lot of
any other American city. It lost more than half
of its population; it lost the whole of its commerce; the great fire of 1776, followed by the
fire of 1778, laid a full fourth of it in ashes; it
was occupied by the enemy uninterruptedly from
almost the beginning of hostilities until after
peace was declared.

When the issue was joined between the colonies and the mother-country, the dominant sentiment here was that of loyalty. This was natural.
In New York, as in the Virginia and Carolina
plantations, the early establishment of large
landed estates had created a class of rich gentlefolk with whom loyalty was a logical instinct.
The abstract convictions, as well as the material

*Plan of the City of* NEW YORK.

Surveyed in the Years 1766 & 1767 by B. RATZEN.

JAS. S. KEMP.

interests, of this class were in favor of the maintenance of royal authority.   It is not surprising, therefore—even in view of the vast stupidities of administration on the part of the home government, which made colonial life almost unendurable — that many an honest gentleman of that period found himself awkwardly tangled in the ethics of honor while deciding between his duty to his country and his duty to his king.   Rather is it surprising that the verdict of the gentle class was given with so little reservation for the patriotic side.   Naturally, also, the commercial class— having vested interests to defend against the perils incident to revolution—was disposed toward loyalty.   At that time about one-tenth of all the foreign commerce of the British-American colonies was centred at this port; the trade inward and outward was increasing steadily and largely; even though the colonies in the end should be successful, a war with England meant an immediate collapse of business and a great money loss.   And yet, with all this daunting loom of disaster—whereof the foreboding was more than justified by the event—no other American city espoused the cause of independence with a blither energy than did New York.

Until the actual outbreak of hostilities, the prosperous expansion of trade and the growth of the city continued without interruption; and then, as suddenly as the coming of tropical night —with the arrival of the British army of occupation, September 15, 1776—a blight settled over everything, and was not lifted for more than seven years.  Only four days after General Howe's entry came the calamity of the great fire : which swept over the region between Whitehall and Broad streets as far north as Beaver; thence, sparing the western side of the Bowling Green, over both sides of Broadway to and including Trinity Church ; and thence, sparing the western side of Broadway, but burning down to the river, to and including the southern side of Vesey Street —leaving behind it a broad furrow of desolation three-quarters of a mile long.  Two years later another fire reduced to wreck almost the whole of the block south of Pearl Street between Coenties and Old slips.  Through all the dreary time of the English occupation these many blocks of ruins remained as the fire had left them.   No reason existed for rebuilding ; and, no matter how strong a reason there might have been, no money for rebuilding was obtainable.  This visible material wreck fittingly represented the wreck which had overtaken the city's most vital interests.  Trade with the interior and coastwise practically was cut off ; and, with the destruction of these its natural feeders, the foreign commerce of the port was dead.

When New York was evacuated by the British troops, November 25, 1783, the condition of the city was miserable to the last degree.  Streets which had been opened and partly graded before the war began had been suffered to lapse again to idle wastes ; the wharves, to which for so long a while no ships had come, had crumbled through neglect; public and private buildings, taken possession of by the military and used as barracks, as hospitals and as prisons, had fallen into semi-ruin; along all the western side of the town was the wreck left by the fire. In this dismal period the population had dwindled from upwards of 20,000 to less than 10,000 souls; the revenues of the city, long uncollected, had shrunk almost to the vanishing-point; the machinery of civil government had been practically destroyed. In a word, without the consoling glory of having suffered in honorable battle, the city was left a wreck by war.

The brilliant rapidity with which New York revived from what seemed to be its dying condition affords a striking proof of its inherent strong vitality. Within three years from the date of the evacuation the former population had been regained, and within five years more a farther increase of 10,000 had made the total 30,000 souls. Commerce, likewise, had returned to and then had passed its former highest limit. Public and private enterprise once more had been fully aroused. In every way the energetic life and the material prosperity of the city had been more than regained.

Before the Revolution, the filling in of the East River front had been carried forward as far as Front Street. Immediately upon the revival of commerce this work was taken in hand again —the more readily because the increasing size of

ships called for deeper water at the wharves—
and South Street was begun.   At the same time,
new streets were laid out to the east and west of
the Bowery; even Broadway, at last, began to
show some signs of becoming an important thoroughfare; the streets leading out of Broadway to
the North River were graded, and some of them
were paved—but this region, then and for a long
while afterward, was the worst quarter of the
town.   What tended, however, most of all to
give to the city an air of fully restored vitality
was the erection of new buildings on the sites so
long covered by the desolate wreckage of the two
fires.

Yet, for all its real prosperity—indeed, because
of its prosperity—the draggled, transitional New
York of that flourishing time must have been a
vastly disagreeable place of residence.   Not only
was it ugly because of its crudeness and its harsh
contrasts; it was a dangerous town to live in because of the frequent presence of epidemic disease.   The prevalence of small-pox—Dr. Jenner's
discovery still being a little below the surface—
was not chargeable to any defect in the crudely
organized system for protecting the public health;
yellow-fever, however, was a practically preventa-
ble disease which, partly through ignorance and
partly through carelessness, was suffered to work
great havoc here.   When "a large and respectable committee of the citizens, of the physicians,
and of the corporation," investigated the cause of
one of the yellow-fever epidemics, about this time,

Plan of the
CITY OF NEW YORK
1767.

Surveyed by
Bernd. Ratzen.

SCALE OF FEET
0    400    1200    2000

they reported that the spread of the fever was en-
couraged (as well it might be !) by " deep damp
cellars, sunken yards, unfinished water lots, public slips containing filth and stagnant water, bur-
ials in the city, narrow and filthy streets, the in-
ducement to intemperance offered by more than
a thousand tippling-houses, and the want of an
adequate supply of pure and wholesome water."

But the New-Yorkers of that day—having great
faith in the glorious future of their city, and being blessed with strong noses and stout hearts—
rose superior to rawness and ugliness and (excepting when they died of them) to pestilence-
breeding bad smells.   Mangin's map, 1803, shows
the extent to which—under the stimulus of a vig-
orously reviving commerce and a rapidly increasing population—they were disposed to discount
their future.   Actually, three-fourths of the im-
pressive-looking city plotted on this map is pure
prophecy : whereof there was but little fulfilment
for near a score of years, and some of it never
was fulfilled at all !   In this brave showing of
projected streets almost the only real streets—
above Anthony and Hester—are those of the little group in the northwest corner, about the State
prison, comprising Greenwich Village.   Brannan
and Bullock streets (the last-named blessedly
changed to Broome, later) were laid out ; the
present Stuyvesant Street, Astor Place, and
Greenwich Avenue were in existence as a continuous system of lanes ; the Amity Street of the
map (not the existing Amity Street) was another

lane—of which a trace still may be seen in the
oblique court leading off from the east side of
South Fifth Avenue below Third Street ; and
Greenwich Street—from Duane northward—was
in existence as the main road to Greenwich, and
was in great vogue as a fashionable drive. All
the rest of these fine-looking streets were but en-
thusiastic projects of what was expected to be in
the fulness of time.

Meanwhile, the tendency of development still
was along the eastern side of the island. The
seat of the foreign trade was the East River
front ; of the wholesale domestic trade, on Pearl
and Broad streets and about Hanover Square ;
of the retail trade, on William, between Fulton
and Wall. Nassau Street and upper Pearl Street
were places of fashionable residence ; as were also
lower Broadway and the Battery. Upper Broadway, paved as far as Warren Street, no longer
was looked upon as remote and inaccessible ; and
people with exceptionally long heads were beginning, even, to talk of it as a street with a future — being thereto moved, no doubt, by consideration of its magnificent appearance as the great
central thoroughfare of the city upon Mangin's
prophetic plan.

The substantial facts of this hopeful period justified a good deal of spread-eagle prophecy. Between the years 1789 and 1801 the duties on foreign goods imported into New York increased
from less than $150,000 to more than $500,000 ;
the exports increased in value from $2,500,000

THE CONFLAGRATION IN 1776

to almost $20,000,000; the tonnage of American vessels in the foreign trade ran up from 18,000 to 146,000, and in the coasting - trade from below 5000 to above 34,000 tons.   In the same period the population had doubled — increasing from 30,000 to 60,000 souls.   While its commerce thus constantly augmented, and while its borders constantly expanded to accommodate its quickly increasing population, New York buzzed with the activity of a vast hive of exceptionally enterprising and successful bees.

## VI

By far the most important improvement belonging to the last decade of the eighteenth century—though one of such magnitude that more than a decade of the nineteenth century had passed before it was completed—was the filling in of the Collect,* or Fresh Water pond.

Primitively, a marshy valley extended across the island from about the present Roosevelt Slip to where now is the western end of Canal Street. Nearly midway in this valley was the Collect: whereof the original outlet was a stream flowing into the East River across the low-lying region which still is called " the Swamp."   As the city advanced up the shore of the East River, the

* The name Collect was a corruption of the Dutch Kalch-hook (meaning lime-shell point), given to a shell-covered promontory above the pond, and later transferred to the pond itself.

Swamp was drained ; and, before the Revolution, the radical improvement was effected of drawing off the overflow of the Collect in the other direction—that is to say, by a drain cut through the marsh, on the line of the present Canal Street, to the North River. But the pond, a barrier in the way of the uniform expansion of the city northward, still remained.

Three principal plans for dealing with the Collect were held under advisement at different times. One was to make a dock of it by cutting navigable canals east and west to the rivers ; another was to use it as a source of water supply for the city ; and still another was to fill it in by cutting down and casting into it the near-by hills. The very great depth of the pond—so great that in early times it was reputed to be bottomless—caused some delay in deciding upon the heroic plan of filling it in ; but eventually, about the end of the last century, this plan was adopted ; and practically was completed in the course of the ensuing ten years.

A good deal of sentiment has been wasted, at one time and another, over the extinction of this little lake. Actually, filling in the Collect was the only possible thing to do with it. To have left it under any conditions—even in the midst of a considerable park and with underground communication with tide-water, which was one of the several suggestions made in the premises— would have resulted in the creation of a fever-trap altogether intolerable : precisely such anoth-

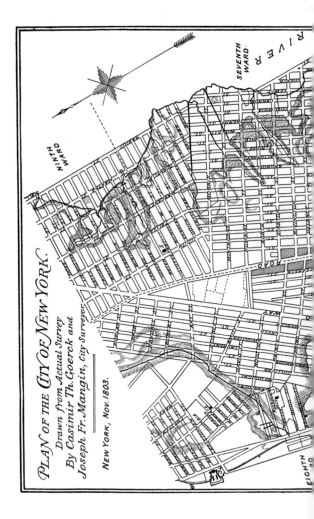

PLAN OF THE CITY OF NEW YORK.

Drawn from Actual Survey
By Casimir Th. Goerck and
Joseph Fr. Mangin, City Surveyors.

NEW YORK, Nov. 1803.

NINTH WARD

SEVENTH WARD

RIVER

EIGHTH

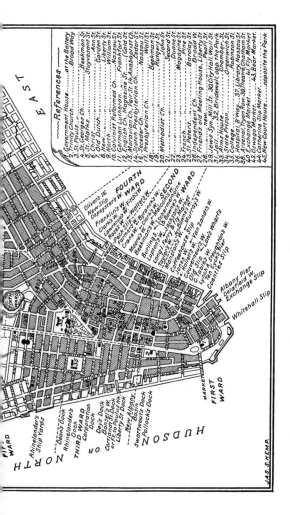

er abiding-place of malaria and bad smells as was the Basin in the city of Providence. But, while the filling in was inevitable, a very great error was committed in using the made land for building sites. Had this unwholesome region been set aside as a public park—abundantly planted with trees which would have sucked up the moisture out of the sodden soil—the city would have made a substantial gain on the double score of beauty and of health.

Before the drainage of the Collect was completed, not only had the seers of that period foreseen the modern city, but a staid and practical Commission—doing for New York precisely what we are laughing at the people of Chicago for causing to be done for their city now—had plotted it, as far north as 155th Street, almost as it exists to-day. Indeed, the prophecies of Mangin's map seemed quite sober realities when compared with the prophecies of the map which the Commissioners produced eight years later, 1811 ; and it is a fact that some parts of the Commissioners' Plan still remain unrealized, although more than eighty years have slipped away since the Plan was made.

As is shown on Mangin's map, the crookedness of the lower part of the city, south of the Fresh Water, was repeated north of the Fresh Water on a grander scale. In this new region the streets were straight in their several groups, but the groups were so defiantly at variance with each other that wherever their edges came to-

gether there was a tangle fit to make a loadstone
lose its way; which picturesque confusion was
due to the fact that each group had started from
a separate base—the shore lines of various parts
of the island, different angles of the line of the
Bowery, and the lines of Broadway and Christopher Street — and thence had extended until,
quite at hazard, they had come together, but had
not joined. However, some part of this tangle
still was only on paper — many of the plotted
streets remaining unopened—and therefore could
be corrected before it became a reality; and all
of the island north of the present Fourteenth
Street practically was virgin territory which could
be treated in whatever way seemed most conducive to the public good. These facts being con-
sidered, the wise conclusion was reached very
early in the present century to correct (so far as
this was possible) the then existing City Plan,
which had been created by a mere patching together of scattered parts for the benefit of private interests, and to make a larger plan — so
comprehensive that the growth of the city for a
century or more would be provided for—in the
interest of the community as a whole.

To make this rational project operative, an act
of Assembly was passed, April 13, 1807, in accordance with the provisions of which Gouverneur Morris, Simeon De Witt, and John Ruther-
ford were appointed "Commissioners of Streets
and Roads in the City of New York," with in-
structions "to lay out streets, roads, and public

squares, of such width [saving that no street should be less than fifty feet wide] and extent as to them should seem most conducive to the public good"; to establish upon the ground the City Plan thus created by the fixing of stone posts at suitable points; and to file maps of the plan with the Secretary of State, the County Clerk, and the Mayor; and the act farther provided that no compensation could be had for buildings destroyed by the opening of streets when it should be shown that such buildings had been erected after the maps had been filed.

The Commissioners, who were allowed four years in which to prepare their plan and to establish it upon the ground, completed their work in outline within that period: in the year 1811 their report was made and their maps were filed which created the city, north of Houston Street, excepting in the matter of public parks, substantially as it exists to-day. The work of exact location — involving the survey of all the streets, and the placing of "1549 marble monumental stones and 98 iron bolts," as is recorded by the minutely accurate Mr. John Randel, Jun., the engineer in charge of the work—was not completed until about the year 1821.

Unfortunately, the promise of this far-sighted undertaking was far from being fulfilled in its performance. The magnificent opportunity which was given to the Commissioners to create a beautiful city simply was wasted and thrown away. Having to deal with a region well wooded, broken by hills, and diversified by water-courses—where the very contours of the land suggested curving roads, and its unequal surface reservations for beauty's sake alone—these worthy men decided that the forests should be cut away, the hills levelled, the hollows filled in, the streams buried; and upon the flat surface thus created they clapped down a ruler and completed their Bœotian programme by creating a city in which all was right angles and straight lines.

These deplorable results were not reached lightly. The Commissioners, in their stolid way, unquestionably gave their very best thought to the work confided to their indiscretion; they even, by their own showing, rose to the height of considering the claims of what they believed to be the beautiful before they decided upon giving place to the useful alone. Appended to their map are what they modestly style " remarks," in the course of which—after stating that they had "personally reconnoitred" the region with which they were dealing — they declare " that one of the first objects which claimed the attention of the Commissioners was the form and manner in which the business should be conducted; that is to say, whether they should confine themselves to rectilinear and rectangular streets, or whether they should adopt some of those supposed improvements by circles, ovals, and stars which certainly embellish a plan, whatever may be their effect as to convenience and utility. In considering that subject they could not but bear in

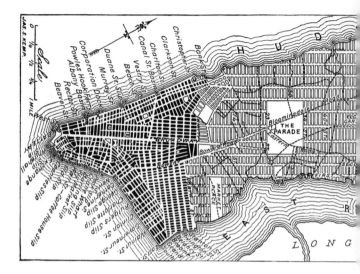

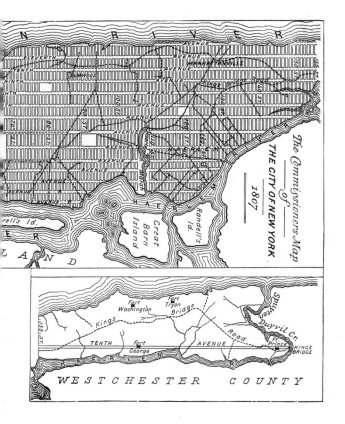

The Commissioners Map
of
THE CITY OF NEW YORK
1807

mind that a city is to be composed principally of the habitations of men, and that straight-sided and right-angled houses are the most cheap to build and the most convenient to live in. The effect of these plain and simple reflections was decisive "— that is to say, the rectangles and straight lines carried the day.

In regard to parks, these excellently dull gentlemen had equally common-sensible views. " It may be a matter of surprise," they write, " that so few vacant spaces have been left, and those so small, for the benefit of fresh air and consequent preservation of health. Certainly if the city of New York was destined to stand on the side of a small stream, such as the Seine or Thames, a great number of ample places might be needful. But those large arms of the sea which embrace Manhattan Island render its situation, in regard to health and pleasure, as well as to the convenience of commerce, peculiarly felicitous. When, therefore, from the same causes, the prices of land are so uncommonly great, it seems proper to admit the principles of economy to greater influence than might, under circumstances of a different kind, have consisted with the dictates of prudence and the sense of duty." Holding these views the Commissioners explained that " it appears proper, nevertheless, to select and set apart on an elevated position a space sufficient for a large reservoir when it shall be found needful to furnish the city, by means of aqueducts or by the aid of hydraulic machinery, with a copious supply of pure and

wholesome water"; and that "it was felt to be in-
dispensable that a much larger space should be set
apart for military exercise, as also to assemble, in
case of need, the force destined to defend the city"
—out of which secondary series of considerations
came the really magnificent Parade, extending from
Twenty-third to Thirty-fourth Street, and from
Fourth to Seventh Avenue, that eventually shrunk
away into the existing Madison Square. The third
large reservation made by the Commissioners, the
space for a great market, never got beyond the
paper plan; which is the more to be regretted
because this particular project, being quite within
the range of their capabilities, was admirably well
conceived. Union Place—now called, very unrea-
sonably, Union Square—was a sort of geographical accident, which in later times has suffered a
great reduction in size. "This Place," wrote the
Commissioners, "becomes necessary from various
considerations. Its central position requires an
opening for the benefit of fresh air; the union of
so many large roads demands space for security
and convenience, and the morsels into which it
would be cut by continuing across it the several
streets and avenues would be of very little use or
value."

The Commissioners, finally, sum up the result
of their labors in these words: "To some it may
be a matter of surprise that the whole island has
not been laid out as a city. To others it may be
a subject of merriment that the Commissioners
have provided space for a greater population

than is collected at any spot on this side of China. They have in this respect been governed by the shape of the ground. It is not improbable that considerable numbers may be collected at Harlem before the high hills to the southward of it shall be built upon as a city; and it is improbable that (for centuries to come) the grounds north of Harlem Flat will be covered with houses. To have come short of the extent laid out might therefore have defeated just expectations; and to have gone further might have furnished materials for the pernicious spirit of speculation."

Excepting in the laying out of the city upon so large a scale—in which there was a touch of uncommon sense that bordered upon imagination—common-sense of the plainest sort was the dominant characteristic of the Commissioners' Plan. Thinking only of utility and economy, they solved their problem—which admitted of so magnificent a solution—in the simplest and dullest way. Yet it is not just to blame them personally because their Plan fell so far short of what might have been accomplished by men of genius governed by artistic taste. All that fairly can be said in the premises — and this quite as much in their justification as to their reproach— is that they were surcharged with the dulness and intense utilitarianism of the people and the period whereof they were a part. Assuredly, the work would have been done with more dash and spirit a whole century earlier—in the slave-dealing and piratical days of New York, when life

here had a flavor of romance in it and was not a
mere grind of money-making in stupid commonplace ways.

Even on the score of utility, however, the Commissioners fell into one very grave error, for
which, the requirements of the case being entirely clear and obvious, there was absolutely no excuse. They were dealing with a long and narrow
island, whereon the strong pressure of traffic nec-
essarily would be longitudinal always. Yet, in
the face of this most obvious fact, their provision
of longitudinal streets was one-third less to the
square mile than was their provision of latitudi-
nal streets; and their case is only made worse by
the existing proof—the greater width of the avenues—that they did dimly recognize the conditions for which they failed to provide. The city
has not yet expanded to the point where the inconvenience arising from this blunder has become
sufficiently marked to attract attention. It will
begin to be felt very soon after the building of
the bridge connecting New York and New Jersey
shall have brought the principal railway lines of
the country into direct connection, on the left
shore of the Hudson, with the principal lines of
foreign steamers, with the resulting transfer to
that region of the commercial centre of the
town.

## VII

While this project of a city, magnificent at least in the matter of size, was in course of elaboration by the serious Commissioners—in the very year, in fact, in which they began their work —the actually existing city of that period had the life temporarily knocked out of it by President Jefferson's Embargo Act: that curious weapon of self-offence which both surprised and annoyed its inventor by going off with such unnecessary violence at the wrong end.

The condition of New York while the deadening effect of the embargo rested upon its commerce was trist to the last degree—as is shown vividly in the following extract, under date of April 13, 1808, from the journal of the exaggerative yet shrewdly observant Mr. John Lambert:

" Everything wore a dismal aspect at New York. The embargo had now continued upwards of three months, and the salutary check which Congress imagined it would have upon the conduct of the belligerent powers was extremely doubtful, while the ruination of the commerce of the United States appeared certain if such destructive measures were persisted in. Already had 120 failures taken place among the merchants and traders, to the amount of more than $5,000,000 ; and there were above 500 vessels in the harbor which were lying up useless, and rotting for want of employment. Thousands of sailors were either destitute of bread wandering about the country, or had entered the British service. The merchants had

shut up their counting - houses and discharged their
clerks; and the farmers refrained from cultivating their
land — for if they brought their produce to market they
could not sell at all, or were obliged to dispose of it for
only a fourth of its value."

In another part of his journal, Lambert wrote:

" The amount of tonnage belonging to the port of New
York in 1806 was 183,671 tons, and the number of vessels
in the harbor on the 25th of December, 1807, when the
embargo took place, was 537. The moneys collected in
New York for the national Treasury, on the imports and
tonnage, have for several years amounted to one-fourth
of the public revenue. In 1806 the sum collected was
$6,500,000, which, after deducting the drawbacks, left a
net revenue of $4,500,000, which was paid into the Treas-
ury of the United States as the proceeds of one year.
In the year 1808 the whole of this immense sum had
vanished!"

Fortunately, it had vanished for only a little
while. Even under the stress of the Non-inter-
course Act, and of the constantly augmenting
political ferment, the commerce of New York revived with such energetic celerity that by the
time war was declared against England, in the
year 1812, the registered tonnage of the port
amounted to 266,548 tons—being equal to that
of Boston and Philadelphia combined, and nearly
double that of any other port in the United
States. Under these circumstances, naturally, the
war bore more heavily upon New York than
upon any other American city; indeed, the reim-
position of the Embargo scarcely would have
produced here a more calamitous result.

A PRIVATEERSMAN ASHORE

The one redeeming feature of the situation, in a business way, was the chance that the war offered for privateering. But even success in this line of spirited endeavor did not yield unalloyed happiness; for privateering had suffered a decided sea-change in the course of the years which had passed since it had been so much the vogue in these parts. It is true that a good many private armed vessels were fitted out from this port during the war of 1812, and it also is true that—to the great profit of their owners—they mowed a fairly broad swath through the English merchant marine. But public sentiment did not unanimously, as in an earlier time, indorse this energetic method of picking up a living on the high seas. Indeed, not very many years later—the more honest view of the matter, meanwhile, having increasingly prevailed — one of our local historians wrote of these very ventures of 1812-15 in the following vigorous terms: "By this legalized piracy a great amount of property belonging to British subjects was plundered at sea and brought into New York; where for a while the enriched freebooters glittered in their ill-gotten splendor, and exerted a most corrupting influence upon society!"

But the enrichment by sea-theft, even to the extent of glittering splendor, of a few freebooting New-Yorkers did not take the place of the more moderate enrichment of all the merchants of the city by legitimate trade. While the war lasted, New York languished miserably. The projects for new streets, the plans for new buildings, were abandoned. So far from increasing, the population actually was lessened by more than two thousand between the years 1810 and 1813. In 1824 the revenues of the port dropped down to but little more than half a million. This was the low-water mark, and in the very next year—peace having been concluded—the revenues shot up to fourteen millions, as foreign goods were poured into the country to make good the long drain. But so violent a revival of business did more harm than good. The vast importations glutted the market, and for six years there was great uncertainty and fluctuation in the state of trade. Not until the third decade of the century was fairly started did commercial balances adjust themselves and a new era of prosperity begin.

During this fluctuating period the growth of the city was spasmodic; but by the year 1820 substantial advances northward had been made. The most important single piece of work in the scheme of development was the completion of the deep canal on the line of Canal Street; with the consequent effective drainage of the whole valley lying between the choked Collect and the North River, and the regulation of the streets, previously laid out, on the reclaimed land. Even before this obstacle had been removed, however, the city had passed beyond it. Soon after the return of peace, building began on Broadway north of "the Meadows," and also near Broadway on Spring and Broome streets — being the

beginning of the movement that twenty years or
so later was to make of this region a highly fashionable quarter of the town.    Even the yellow
fever of 1822––the last of the serious epidemics
of this disease—tended to accelerate the growth
of the city northward, for many of the exiles from
the lower part of the island retained their suburban homes after the fever had passed.    By the
year 1824—in which year " more than 1600 new
houses were erected, nearly all of them of brick
or stone," as is proudly stated by a contemporary
chronicler—the lines of the city blocks were advancing close upon Greenwich Village, and Greenwich itself was becoming a populous suburban
ward.    At the same time a considerable settlement was asserting itself westward of the Bowery.
Between these extremes the building of handsome
villas was giving a vastly aristocratical air to the
heretofore desert reaches of upper Broadway; and
in order to invite the farther expansion of this
fashionable quarter the old Potter's Field was reclaimed from a wilderness, and then — with the
paupers still *in situ* — was transformed into the
present Washington Square.    By the year 1820
the population of the city had increased to 123,-
706 souls.

## VIII

New York's destiny as a commercial centre was
settled from the start by the fact that the city—
therein possessing what all other cities on the

Atlantic seaboard lacked—had ample channels of communication with the interior by water.

Without examining closely a large map, it is not easy to estimate how great an extent of territory—down the whole range of coast from the Connecticut to the Shrewsbury River, and remotely inland—can be reached in perfect safety from this city in a sloop of 20 tons. And in our days of railroads it is even less easy to realize that some of these waterways — the Hackensack, for instance — ever could have been of any serious value to the commerce of New York. But before cheap and speedy means of land carriage had been established every one of these small streams —down to those on which even a 10-ton sloop would float—was a channel of trade which appreciably added to the revenues of this town. It was, therefore, as the direct result of the advantages possessed by New York as a centre of domestic distribution that the city gained the leading place in the foreign trade of North America and acquired a registered tonnage of more than 260,000 tons by the beginning of the war of 1812.

But not until after this war was ended did the business conditions here justify the establishment of regular transatlantic lines with fixed dates of sailing — the famous lines of Liverpool packets, for which some few people of old-fashioned tendencies sigh a little as they take passage nowadays in a record-breaking "greyhound": with the full knowledge that that nondescript and far too spirited animal actually is a frightfully overcrowd-

DEPARTURE OF BLACK BALL AND DRAMATIC PACKETS

ed and badly kept summer-resort hotel got away to sea.

The pioneer establishment in the Liverpool service was the Black Ball Line, started in the year 1817 by Isaac Wright and Son, Francis Thompson, Benjamin Marshal, and Jeremiah Thompson, with four large ships—as ships went, in those days; that is to say, vessels of between 400 and 500 tons —named the *Pacific*, *Amity*, *William Thompson*, and *James Cropper*, with sailing dates fixed for the first day of each month throughout the year. Four years later, when the business of the country was in an unusually flourishing condition, a second line, the Red Star, was established; also with four ships making monthly departures, but sailing on the 24th of the month. In the same year the Black Ball Line put on four more vessels, sailing on the 16th of the month; and a little later the Swallow-tail Line was started, with four ships, making monthly departures on the 8th. Thus communication was established between New York and Liverpool by a fleet of sixteen vessels, making from each end of the line weekly departures the year round. Later, regular lines were established to London, Havre, Greenock, and other European ports; while the increase in the coastwise service naturally kept pace with that of the foreign trade.

The point to be here observed is that the weekly service to and from Liverpool—significant of a very great commercial pressure for that period— was established before the natural advantages

possessed by New York as a distributing centre
had received any artificial improvement ; before,
indeed, any improvement at all had been effected
beyond the opening inland from the various wa-
tercourses of ways more or less practicable for
freight-wagons and pack-trains. It was, therefore,
the demand for the extension of a great business
already soundly established which led to the creation of what frequently has been styled the foun-
dation-stone of New York's commercial supremacy — the Erie Canal. In view of the natural
geographical advantages possessed by this city,
and of the intelligent fostering of trade in the
early times by the grants of staple right and of
the monopoly of flour, it seems a fair inference
that this so - called foundation - stone was set in
when the building had got up to about the third
or fourth floor. But as to the vast importance of
the canal to the well - being of New York—without regard to the structural period at which its
benefits became operative—there can be no question at all. Again it is necessary to examine care-
fully a large map in order to arrive at an adequate
comprehension of what was done for this city
when a waterway was cut from the Hudson River
to the Great Lakes.

This large project was not conceived in its en-
tirety : it was an evolution. In the year 1792,
under the presidency of General Philip Schuyler,
the Western Inland Lock Navigation Company
was incorporated for the purpose of opening a
communication by canal to Seneca Lake and

Lake Ontario and of improving the Mohawk
River. Later, at the suggestion of Gouverneur
Morris—who in this matter worked for the welfare
of the city with an intelligent zeal which he certainly did not manifest when he was helping to
lay it out as a checker-board—the grander plan
was taken into consideration of opening a canal
from the Hudson River to Lake Erie. In the
same year that this statesmanlike suggestion was
made, 1808, the project was brought before the
Assembly by Joshua Forman; an appropriation
was granted for a preliminary survey, and the survey was made by James Geddes. The matter
then dropped for a year, but was revived energet-
ically in March, 1810 — at which time Senator,
afterward Governor, De Witt Clinton became associated with it, and thereafter remained its most
efficient promoter until the successful end.

For several years the war then going on with
England prevented the prosecution of the work;
and even after this military matter had been sat-
isfactorily disposed of (it was rather a brilliant
little war, so far as we were concerned, with some
beautiful fighting in it) the disordered finances of
the country caused still longer delay. Not until
April 17, 1817, was the whole plan solidified into
a legislative act—by which funds were provided
for the construction of a canal 363 miles in length,
with a surface width of 40 feet, a bottom width
of 18 feet, and a water channel 4 feet in depth.
But when the start fairly had been made the work
went ahead rapidly. Ground was broken that

same year, on July 4th, at Rome, on the middle
section ; and the excavation and structural work
were pushed with such diligence that the canal was
opened for traffic in but little more than eight years.

A picturesque celebration of " the wedding of
the waters " followed the completion of the work.
On the morning of October 26, 1825, the first flotilla of canal - boats bound for the seaboard left
Buffalo, starting at the signal of a cannon fired
at the Erie in - take. This shot straightway was
echoed—guns having been stationed at regular intervals—down the whole length of the new waterway, and thence onward down the Hudson to
New York ; where, precisely one hour and twenty-
five minutes after the first gun had been fired beside the lake, the last gun was fired beside the sea.
During another hour and twenty-five minutes the
answer from the ocean to the inland waters went
thundering onward into the northwest.

And then, at this end of the line, the enthusi-
asm aroused in so thrilling a fashion had a whole
fortnight in which to cool while the boats were
crawling eastward. Yet crawling is a dull word
to apply to what really was a triumphal progress.
It would be more in harmony with the oratorical
spirit of the occasion to say that the boats came
eastward on the crest of a wave of popular rejoicing : while all the canal towns burst forth into
speeches of glorification by the lips of their local
dignitaries, and listened to like speeches from
Governor Clinton and Gouverneur Morris and the
other migrant statesmen aboard the flotilla ; while

"ERIE," OCTOBER 26, 1825

flags were flying everywhere by day and bonfires
were blazing everywhere by night; and while all
central New York was vibrant with the uncon-
trolled violence of countless brass bands.

At five o'clock on the morning of November
4th this fresh-water cyclone completed the last
stage of its eventful progress, the run down the
Hudson in tow of the *Chancellor Livingston*, and
halted off the State Prison (at the foot of the
present West Tenth Street), while all the bells
went off into joy-peals and there was a noble bel-
lowing of guns. Off the State Prison (a trysting-
place which aroused no disagreeable doubts and
dreads in the breasts of the aldermen of that earlier, non-boodling day) the flotilla was met by a
deputation of the civic authorities charged with
the duty of "congratulating the company on their
arrival from Lake Erie," and of conducting them
down stream, around the Battery, and up the East
River to the Navy-yard; where a thunderous official salute was fired, and the officers of the corporation welcomed the distinguished guests in form.
And then, from the Navy-yard, "a grand procession, consisting of nearly all the vessels in port
gayly decked with colors of all nations," went
down to the lower bay: where Governor Clinton,
from the deck of the United States schooner
*Dolphin*, about which all the other vessels were
grouped in a great circle, poured a libation of the
fresh water brought from Lake Erie into the salt
water of the Atlantic Ocean—and so typified the
joining together of the inland and the outland seas.

Either in dramatic effect or in commercial im
portance, the only other event in our national history that can be compared with this is the meeting—forty-four years later—of the locomotives at
Promontory Point; and the comparison is the
more seemly because the building of the waterway from the Hudson to the lakes was one of the
most important of the many acts of preparation
which in the fulness of time made the building of
the railway from ocean to ocean possible.


IX


Practically, the building of the Erie Canal completed the material evolution of New York. That
is to say, by the year 1825 the essential elements
were assembled—a large and mixed population,
transportation facilities into the heart of the continent, a foreign trade diffused over the whole
globe—which constitute the New York of to-day.
This is far from saying that the city then entered upon, and ever since has continued in the
possession of, unalloyed prosperity. Being essentially human, New York has a handsome potentiality of error and a fair average liability to mis-
fortune — both of which attributes have been
manifested repeatedly during the past threescore
and eight years. In the way of misfortunes, for
instance, a most serious one came only ten years
after the canal was opened: "the great fire" of
December, 1835, which began near the foot of

Maiden Lane, burned upwards of six hundred buildings, including the Custom-house and the Merchants' Exchange, and caused a money loss of about twenty millions of dollars; some of which painful facts may be seen recorded to this day on a marble tablet displayed upon the building No. 80 Pearl Street. And in the way of errors, one of great magnitude was committed in this same fourth decade of the century—being an error in which the whole country had a share— when the naïve attempt was made to create unlimited credit on the alchemistic basis of paper declared to be transmuted into gold. The fire of 1835, with its vast consumption of substantial wealth, had its share in precipitating the financial panic of 1836–37; but this same panic surely would have come, and only a little later, even had there been no fire at all. Unfortunately, the lesson of 1837 was utterly wasted, and so also have been wasted the similar lessons of later date; for the disposition to dabble in that form of occult chemistry which seeks to create something out of nothing is so profoundly rooted in the human race that it needs must keep on sprouting until the very end of time.

But while on broad lines the material evolution of New York was completed in 1825, the practical development of the existing city dates from that very year. At that time the population numbered only 166,000, and the utmost stretch of fancy could not carry the limits of the city proper above Fourteenth Street. Since then the whole

of the dwelling portion of New York—excepting
comparatively small areas on the east and west
sides of the island—has been created anew; and
within the same period the region below Fourteenth Street, with the exceptions noted, has been
turned over to business purposes, and a great part
of it has been rebuilt—notably that portion lying
south of where once was the wall—in a fashion
that would make the sometime owners of the cab-
bage patches thereabouts use strong Dutch language expressive of awe! In this period, too,
almost everything has been added to New York
which distinguishes a city from an overgrown
town : an adequate and wholesome water supply;
an effective system of lighting ; a provision of
public parks so ample and so magnificently costly
that 'tis fit to make the bones of the economical
Commissioners of 1807 rattle a protest in their
graves. And also—though these be sore and delicate points to touch upon — something has been
done towards providing local transportation, towards properly paving the streets, and even towards
keeping the streets clean. All of these improvements, with the others like in kind but less in degree which subsequently came to pass, were in
embryo in the year 1825 and needed for their development only favoring conditions and time.

Equally existent in embryo were the develop-
ments which were to take place outside of New
York, but which were to be the very corner-stones
of the city's later prosperity : the land and sea
transportation service by steam. The ocean ser-

vice came naturally, in sequence to that which had been expanded to great proportions before the new motive power had been reduced to practical working shape. Being established, the steamship lines had only to grow with the always growing trade. The existing railway service, which makes New York the seaboard terminus of all east-and-west lines, also is the necessary outgrowth of the earlier conditions: when this port alone provided ample facilities for ocean carriage to all parts of the world. Possessing this advantage, the opening of the Erie Canal—a clear ten years before railways began seriously to modify the conditions of trade—gave this city a hold upon the business of the interior of the country that never afterwards was lost. And, consequently, when the railway building began in good earnest there was no question as to which of the seaboard cities should be the objective point of the traffic by rail. Whether the lines ended nominally at Baltimore or Philadelphia or Boston, their actual end—to which most of the goods for export must be brought, and from which almost all foreign goods must be received—was New York.

# GREENWICH VILLAGE

## I

N the resolute spirit of another Andorra, the village of Greenwich maintains its independence in the very midst of the city of New York—submitting to no more of a compromise in the matter of its autonomy than is involved in the Procrustean sort of splicing which has hitched fast the extremities of its tangled streets to the most readily available streets in the City Plan. The flippant carelessness with which this apparent union has been effected only serves to emphasize the actual separation. In almost every case these ill‑advised couplings are productive of anomalous disorder, while in the case of the numbered streets they openly travesty the requirements of communal propriety and of common‑sense: as may be inferred from the fact that within this disjointed region Fourth Street crosses Tenth, Eleventh, and Twelfth streets very nearly at right angles — to the permanent bewilderment of nations and to the perennial confusion of mankind.

In addition to being hopelessly at odds with the surrounding city, Greenwich is handsomely at variance with itself. Its streets, so far as they can be said to be parallel at all, are parallel in four distinct groups; they have a tendency to sidle away from each other and to take sudden and unreasonable turns; some of them start out well enough but, after running only a block or two, encounter a church or a row of houses and pull up short. Here, in a word, is the same sort of irregularity that is found in the lower part of the city between Broadway and the East River, and it comes from the same cause: neither of these crooked regions was a creation; both were growths. As streets were wanted in Greenwich they were opened—or were made by promoting existing lanes—in accordance with the notions of the owners of the land; and that the village did grow up in this loose and easy fashion is indicative of its early origin. Actually, excepting the immediate vicinity of the Battery, this is the oldest habitation of white men on the Island of New York.

But there were red men living here before the white men came. In the Dutch Records references are made to the Indian village of Sappokanican; and this name, or the Bossen Bouerie— meaning farm in the woods — was applied for more than a century to the region which came to be known as Greenwich in the later, English, times. The Indian village probably was near the site of the present Gansevoort Market; but the name seems to have been applied to the whole region lying between the North River and the stream called the Manetta Water or Bestavaar's Kill.

Although the Manetta Creek no longer is visible on the surface, it still flows in diminished volume through its ancient channel—as those living near or over it sometimes know to their cost. Its east branch rises east of the Fifth Avenue between Twentieth and Twenty-first streets, whence it flows in nearly a straight line to the southwest corner of Union Square; thence in a slightly curving line to a junction with the west branch (which rises east of the Sixth Avenue, between Fifteenth and Sixteenth streets) near the middle of the block bounded by Eleventh and Twelfth streets and the Fifth and Sixth avenues; from this junction it flows to the Fifth Avenue and Clinton Place; and thence across Washington Square, through Minetta Street, and nearly parallel with Downing Street, to the North River between Charlton and Houston streets. Notwithstanding the fact that this creek has been either culverted over or filled in throughout its entire length, it still asserts itself occasionally with a most undesirable vigor. Heavy buildings cannot be erected on or near its bed without recourse to a costly foundation of piling or grillage, nor can deep excavations be made anywhere

N. E. CORNER GREENWICH AND TENTH STREETS, 1892

near its channel without danger of overflow. Both of these conditions have been in evidence recently—the pile-driving for the Lincoln Building at the southwest corner of Union Square, and the grillage for the building at the northeast corner of Nineteenth Street and the Fifth Avenue ; the inundation, in the deep cellar lately dug on the Sixth Avenue a little below Eleventh Street, and also in the cellar of the new building No. 66 Fifth Avenue.

In primitive times the land between Manetta Water and the North River was very fertile—a light loamy soil, the value of which anybody with half an eye for soils could see at a glance. Wherefore Peter Minuit, first of the Dutch governors, with a becoming regard for the interests of his owners—this was just after he had bought the whole Island of Manhattan from the unsuspecting savages for sixty guilders, or twenty-four dollars—set apart Sappokanican as one of the four farms to be reserved to the Dutch West India Company in perpetuity. With even greater, but more personal, astuteness the second Dutch Governor, Wouter Van Twiller—having a most unbecoming regard for his own strictly individual interests—made himself at once grantor and grantee of this property, and so appropriated the Company's Farm No. 3 as his own private tobacco plantation. He was a weak brother, this Governor Van Twiller, and his governing was of a spasmodic and feeble sort ; but his talent for converting public property to private uses was so

marked that it would have given him prominence
at a very much later period in the history of the
Ninth Ward—the whole of which section of the
future city, it will be observed, with some considerable slices from the adjacent territory, he
grabbed with one swoop of his big Dutch hands.

Van Twiller, coming over in the *Southberg*,
landed on this island in April, 1633. As he was
dilatory only in matters of state it is reasonable
to suppose that he annexed Sappokanican in time
to sow his first crop of tobacco that very year.
His farm - house doubtless was the first house
erected on the island of Manhattan north of the
settlement around Fort Amsterdam; and with
the building of this house at the Bossen Bouerie,
Greenwich Village was founded — only a dozen
years after the formal colonization of the New
Netherland, and rather more than two centuries
and a half ago.

Things went so easily and gently in those placid
times that a long while passed before the Bossen
Bouerie suffered the smallest change. Twenty
years later, in the time of Governor Stuyvesant,
mention is made of "the few houses at Sappo-
kanigan"; and nearly half a century later a passing reference to the settlement there is made in
the Labadist journal so fortunately discovered by
the late Henry C. Murphy during his residence
at the Hague. Under date of September 7, 1679,
the journal contains this entry: "We crossed over
the island, which takes about three-quarters of an
hour to do, and came to the North River, which

ON THE STEPS

we followed a little within the woods to Sapokan-
ikee. Gerrit having a sister and friends there, we
rested ourselves and drank some good beer, which
refreshed us. We continued along the shore to
the city, where we arrived at an early hour in the
evening, very much fatigued, having walked this
day about forty miles. I must add, in passing
through this island we sometimes encountered
such a sweet smell in the air that we stood still;
because we did not know what it was we were
meeting."

And so for about a century after Governor Van
Twiller, in a prophetically aldermanic fashion, had
boodled to himself the whole of the future Ninth
Ward, the settlement at the Bossen Bouerie, otherwise Sappokanican, was but a hamlet, and a very
small hamlet, tucked into the edge of the woodland a little to the northward of where the docks
of the Cunard and White Star steamers were to be
in the fulness of time: and the hamleters doubtless had very fine trout-fishing between the future
Fifth and Sixth avenues in the Manetta Water;
and, in the autumn, good duck-shooting over the
marsh which later was to be Washington Square.


II


I know not how long a time may have elapsed
between the conquest of this island by the English and the discovery by the Dutch living retired
at the Bossen Bouerie that, a sea-change having

overswept their destinies, they had passed from
the domination of the States General to the domination of the British King.

It is said that when the engineers of the West
Shore Railroad, provided with guides and inter-
preters, penetrated into the valley of the Hackensack, a dozen years or so ago, they created a great
commotion among the honest Dutch folk dwelling in those sequestered parts by taking in the
news that something more than eighty years previously the American Republic had been pro-
claimed.   Some few of the more wide-awake of
these retired country folk had got hold, it was found,
of a rumor to the effect that the New Netherland,
having been traded away for Surinam by the provisions of the Treaty of Breda, had become a dependency of the British crown ; but the rumor
never had been traced to an authoritative source,
and was regarded by the older and more conserv-
ative of the inhabitants of Tenafly and Schraalen-
burg and Kinderkamack, and the towns thereto
adjacent, as mere idle talk.   Naturally, the much
more impossible story told by the engineers involved so violent a strain upon human credulity
that the tellers of it were lucky in getting safely
away, across the hills by Rockland Lake to the
Hudson Valley, with unbroken theodolites and
whole hides.   The matter, I may add, is reported
to have remained in uncertainty until the running of milk-trains over the new railroad brought
this region into communication with the outside
world.

The case of the people dwelling at Sappokanican was different. This hamlet being less remote, and far less inaccessible, than the towns in the Hackensack Valley — being, indeed, but a trifle more than two miles northward of the Dutch stronghold—there is reason for believing that the news of the surrender of Fort Amsterdam to the English, on the 8th of September, 1664, penetrated

NO. 54 DOWNING STREET

thither within a comparatively short period after the gloomy event occurred. Indeed—while there is no speaking with absolute precision in this matter—I can assert confidently that within but a trifle more than half a century after the change of rulers had taken place the inhabitants of this settlement were acquainted with what had occurred : as is proved by an existing land conveyance, dated 1721, in which the use of the phrase "the Bossen Bouerie, alias Greenwich," shows not only that the advent of the English was known there, but that already the new-comers had so wedged themselves into prominence as to begin their mischievous obliteration of the good old Dutch names.

For a long while I cherished the belief that the name of Greenwich had been given to the Bossen Bouerie by a gallant sailor who for a time made that region his home : Captain Peter Warren of the Royal Navy — who died Sir Peter Warren, K.B., and a Vice-Admiral of the Red Squadron, and whose final honor was a tomb in the Abbey in the company of other heroes and of various kings. Applied by a British sailor to his home ashore, there was an absolute fitness in the name; and it had precisely a parallel in the bestowal of the name of Chelsea upon the adjoining estate by a soldier, Colonel Clarke. But a considerate survey of the facts has compelled me, though very reluctantly, to abandon this pleasingly poetical hypothesis. I am inclined to believe that the name Greenwich was in use by or before the year

SIR PETER WARREN K.B.

Vice Admiral of the Red Squadron

(From *The Naval Chronicle* for October, 1804.)

1711, at which time Peter Warren was a bog-trotting Irish lad of only eight years old; and it certainly was in use, as is proved by the land conveyance cited above, as early as the year 1721, at which time my gentleman was but a sea-lieutenant, and had not (so far as I can discover) laid eyes on America at all.

Admiral Sir Peter Warren was a dashing personage in his day and generation, but his glory was won in what now are wellnigh forgotten wars. Irish by birth, and with as fine a natural disposition for fighting as ever an Irishman was blessed with, he worked his way up in the service with so handsome a rapidity that he was gazetted a post-captain, and to the command of his Majesty's ship *Grafton*, when he was only twenty-four years old—and his very first service after being posted was in the fleet with which Sir Charles Wager knocked the Rock of Gibraltar loose from the rest of the Spanish possessions; and thereafter, with more rigor than righteousness, annexed it to the dominions of the British Crown.

This was in the year 1727. In the year 1728 Captain Warren was on the American station in the *Solebay*, frigate; probably was here again in 1737; and certainly was here from about 1741 until 1746 in the *Squirrel*, sloop, the *Launceston*, frigate, and the 60-gun ship *Superbe*. In the spring of 1744 Sir Chaloner Ogle left him for a while commodore of a squadron of sixteen sail on the Leeward Islands station—where his luck so well stood by him that off Martinique, in but little more than four months (February 12–June 24) the ships of his squadron captured no less than twenty-four prizes: one of which was a register-ship whereof the lading of plate was valued at £250,000!

Most of these prizes were sent into New York to be condemned; and " Messieurs Stephen De Lancey & Company " (as appears from an advertisement in *The Weekly Post Boy* for June 30, 1744) acted as the agents of Captain Warren in the sale of his French and Spanish swag. Naturally, the good bargains to our merchants which came of his dashing performances made him vastly popular here. After his brilliant cruise he returned to New York that the *Launceston* might " go upon the careen "; and when he had refitted and was about to get to sea again the *Post Boy* (August 27) gave him this fine send-off: " His Majesty's ship *Launceston*, commanded by the brave Commodore Warren (whose absence old Oceanus seems to lament), being now sufficiently repaired, will sail in a few Days in order once more to pay some of his Majesty's enemies a Visit.

> " ' The sails are spread ; see the bold warrior comes
> To chase the French and interloping Dons !' "

Of my commodore's gallant work at Louisburg (for which the violent Mr. Dunlap refuses to give him a particle of credit), and of his gallant share (about which there can be no question) in the action fought by Anson with the French off Cape

WARREN MONUMENT, WESTMINSTER ABBEY

Finisterre on the 3d of May, 1747, I cannot properly write in this place ; nor can I here do more for his memory than make bare mention of the fact that he sat in Parliament for the city of Westminster during the last few years of his life. But 'tis plain that a naval personage so eminent fairly deserved—when his cruising on this planet was ended and he was ordered to that higher station which he had earned by his heroic virtues while on earth: as the case would have been stated in the phrasing of his time — something out of the common in the way of an enduring memorial. And he certainly got it. In *The Naval Chronicle* I find recorded the fact that " A superb monument was erected to his memory in Westminster Abbey, which was executed by that great master of his time, Roubiliac. Against the wall is a large flag hanging to the flag-staff, and spreading in natural folds behind the whole monument. In the front is a fine figure of Hercules placing Sir Peter's bust on its pedestal, and on one side is a figure of Navigation, with a wreath of laurel in her hand, gazing on the bust with a look of melancholy mixt with admiration "—and so on.

In his *Historical Memorials of Westminster Abbey*, Dean Stanley writes: " In the North Transept and the north aisle of the Choir follow the cenotaphs of a host of seamen," among which is that of " Warren, represented by Roubiliac with the marks of the small-pox on his face." The Dean adds that Roubiliac " constantly visited Dr.

Johnson to get from him epitaphs worthy of his works"; and therefore concludes, as also from the strong internal evidence, that the following high-flowing effusion is from the Doctor's pen:

Sacred to the memory
of Sir PETER WARREN,
Knight of the Bath,
Vice-Admiral of the Red Squadron
of the British Fleet,
and Member of Parliament
For the City and Liberty of Westminster.

He Derived his Descent from an Antient Family of
IRELAND;
His Fame and Honours from his Virtues and Abilities.
How eminently these were displayed,
With what vigilance and spirit they were exerted,
In the various services wherein he had the honour
To command,
And the happiness to conquer,
Will be more properly recorded in the Annals of
GREAT BRITAIN.
On this tablet Affection with truth must say
That, deservedly esteemed in private life,
And universally renowned for his public conduct,
The judicial and gallant Officer
Possessed all the amiable qualities of the
Friend, the Gentleman, and the Christian:
But the ALMIGHTY,
Whom alone he feared, and whose gracious protection
He had often experienced,
Was pleased to remove him from a place of Honour,
To an eternity of happiness,
On the 29th day of July, 1752,
In the 49th year of his age.

## III

I have revived for a moment the personality
of this "judicial and gallant Officer" because the
village of Greenwich, while not named by him,
had its rise on one of the estates which he purchased with his winnings at sea.

Flying his flag aboard the *Launceston*, commanding on the station, and making such a brave
show with his captured ships, Captain—by courtesy Commodore — Warren cut a prodigiously
fine figure here in New York about the year of
grace 1744; so fine, indeed, that never a man in
the whole Province, excepting only the Governor,
could be compared with him in dignity. And
under these brilliant circumstances it is not at
all surprising that pretty Mistress Susannah De
Lancey was quite ready to complete his tale of
"Irishman's luck" by giving him in her own
sweet person an heiress for a wife; nor that her
excellent father—who already must have made a
pot of money out of this most promising son-in-
law—was more than ready to give his consent to
the match. It was about the time of the Commodore's marriage, probably, that he bought his
Greenwich farm—a property of not far from three
hundred acres; which was a little increased, later, by a gift of land voted to him by the city
in recognition of his achievement at Louisburg
in 1745.

Pending the building of his country-seat, and probably also as a winter residence, Captain Warren occupied the Jay house near the lower end of Broadway. One of the historians of New York, falling violently afoul of another historian of New York, has asserted hotly that Captain Warren built and lived in the house, known as the Kennedy house, which long occupied the site No. 1 Broadway. Heaven forbid that I should venture to thrust my gossiping nose (if so bold a metaphor may be tolerated) into this archæological wrangle; but, with submission, it is necessary for my present purposes to assert positively that Captain Warren had no more to do with the building of the Kennedy house than he had to do with the building of the Tower of Babel. In the English Records, under date of May, 1745, is this entry: "Ordered: That a straight line be drawn from the south corner of the house of Mr. Augustus Jay, now in the occupation of Peter Warren, Esquire, to the north corner of the house of Archibald Kennedy, fronting the Bowling Green in Broadway, and that Mr. William Smith, who is now about to build a house (and all other persons who shall build between the two houses) lay their foundations and build conformably to the aforesaid line." This record, I conceive, fixes definitely Captain Warren's downtown residence, and also sufficiently confirms the accepted genesis of the Kennedy house.

Concerning the country-seat at Greenwich even the historians have not very materially disagreed.

A STAGE IN THE THIRTIES

It was built by Captain Warren on a scale of elegance appropriate to one who had only to drop across to the Leeward Islands and pick up a Spanish plate-ship, or a few French West-Indiamen, in order to satisfy any bills which the carpenters and masons might send in; and the establishment seems to have been maintained upon a footing of liberality in keeping with this easy way of securing a revenue. The house stood about three hundred yards back from the river, on ground which fell away in a gentle slope towards the waterside. The main entrance was from the east; and at the rear—on the level of the drawing-room and a dozen feet or so above the sloping hill-side—was a broad veranda commanding the view westward to the Jersey Highlands and southward down the bay clear to the Staten Island hills. I like to fancy my round little captain seated upon this veranda, of placid summer afternoons, smoking a comforting pipe after his mid-day dinner; and taking with it, perhaps, as sea-faring gentlemen very often did in those days, a glass or two of substantial rum-and-water to keep everything below hatches well stowed. With what approving eyes must he have regarded the trimly kept lawns and gardens below him; and with what eyes of affection the *Launceston*, all a-taunto, lying out in the stream! Presently, doubtless, the whiffs from his pipe came at longer and longer intervals, and at last entirely ceased —as the spirit which animated his plumply prosperous body, lulled by its soft and mellowing surroundings, sank gently into peaceful sleep. And then I fancy him, an hour or two later, wakened by Mistress Sue's playing upon the harpsichord; and his saying handsome things to her (in his rich Irish brogue) when she comes from the drawing-room to join him, and they stand together—one of his stout little arms tucked snugly about her jimp waist—looking out across the gleaming river, and the Elysian Fields dark in shadow, at the

THE WARREN HOUSE, GREENWICH

glowing splendor of the sunset above the foot-hills of the Palisades.

The picture of the house which is here repro-duced was made a hundred years after the admi-ral had ceased to cruise upon the waters of this planet, and when the property was in the posses-sion of the late Abraham Van Nest, Esq.—whose home it was for more than thirty years. Great locust-trees stood guard about it, together with a few poplars; and girding the garden were thick hedges of box, whence came in the summer days of hot sunshine—as I am told by one of the de-lightful old gentlemen with whom of late I have been holding converse—a sweetly aromatic smell. The poplar - trees, probably, dated from the first decade of the present century, at which period they had an extraordinary vogue. It was in the year 1809 that Mr. Samuel Burling's highly inju-dicious offer to plant with poplar-trees the princi-pal street of New York — from Leonard Street northward to the Greenwich Lane—was accepted gratefully by the corporation, " because it will be an additional beauty to Broadway, the pride of our city"; and the outcome of that particular piece of beautifying was to make Broadway look for a great many years afterwards like a street which had escaped from a Noah's ark!

But long before anybody had even dreamed that the Broadway ever would be extended to these remote northern regions the Warren farm had passed from the possession not only of Sir Peter, but also from the possession of his three

daughters—Charlotte, Ann, and Susannah—who
were his only children and heirs. The admiral
seems to have been but little in America during
the later years of his life; and after 1747—when
he was elected a member of Parliament for the
city of Westminster—I find no authentic trace of
him on this side of the Atlantic. But Lady Warren, while Sir Peter was spending the most of his
time at sea, blazing away with his cannon at the
French, very naturally continued to reside near
her father and brother here in New York; not
until his election to Parliament, at which time
he became a householder in London, did she join
him on the other side.

Doubtless, also, consideration for her daughters
—in the matter of schooling, and with a look ahead
towards match-making—had much to do with her
ladyship's move. So far as match-making was
concerned, the change of base enabled her to
make a very fair score — two, out of a possible
three. Charlotte, the eldest daughter, married
Willoughby, Earl of Abingdon; and Ann, the second daughter, married Charles Fitzroy, afterward
Baron Southampton: whereby is seen that real
estate in New York, coupled with a substantial
bank account, gave as firm assurance of a coronet
sevenscore years ago as it does to-day. Susannah,
the youngest daughter, was indiscreet enough, I
fear, to make a mere love-match. She married a
paltry colonel of foot, one William Skinner—and
presently died, as did also her husband, leaving behind her a baby Susannah to inherit her

third of the chunky admiral's prize-moneys and lands.

The names of the husbands of all three of these ladies became attached to the property in New York. Skinner Road was the present Christopher Street; Fitzroy Road ran north, near the line of the present Eighth Avenue, from about the present Fourteenth Street to about the present Forty-second Street; the Southampton Road ran from the present Gansevoort Street (which was a part of it) diagonally to a point on the Abingdon Road, a little east of the present Sixth Avenue; and the Abingdon Road (called also Love Lane), practically on the line of the present Twenty-first Street, connected what now is Broadway with the Fitzroy Road, and eventually was extended to the North River. The only survival of any of these family names is in Abingdon Square.

The deeds for the property in the Greenwich region all begin by reciting—with the old-womanly loquacity of deeds—the facts in regard to Sir Peter's issue briefly set forth above; and in addition tell how his estate was partitioned by a process in which the solemnity of legal procedure was mitigated by an agreeable dash of the dicing habits of the day: "In pursuance of the powers given in the said antenuptial deeds the trustees therein named, on March 31, 1787, agreed upon a partition of the said lands, which agreement was with the approbation and consent of the cestui que trusts, to wit: Earl and Lady Abingdon, and Charles Fitzroy and Ann his wife, the said Susan-

nah Skinner the second not then having arrived
at age. In making the partition, the premises
were divided into three parts on a survey made
thereof and marked A, B, and C; and it was
agreed that such partition should be made by each
of the trustees naming a person to throw dice
for and in behalf of their respective cestui que
trusts, and that the person who should throw the
highest number should have parcel A; the one
who should throw the next highest number should
have parcel B; and the one who should throw
the lowest number should have parcel C—for the
persons whom they respectively represented; and
the premises were partitioned accordingly."

It was on the lines of the map made for this
partition that Greenwich went along easily and
peacefully until it was brought up with a round
turn, in the year 1811, by the formation of the
present City Plan.

## IV

The lots into which the Warren property was
divided were of twelve or fifteen acres, suitable
for small farms or country-seats, and the base-
line naturally adopted was the present Greenwich Avenue, then Monument Lane. By the
turn of the dice, the homestead, with fifty-five
acres of land round about it, fell to the share of
Lady Abingdon; who united with her husband
in selling it, in 1788, for $2200. A little later the
property passed into the possession of Abijah

A WISTARIA WALK, HORATIO STREET

Hammond; and from him the mansion-house, with the square bounded by Fourth, Bleecker, Perry, and Charles streets, was purchased by Mr. Van Nest, in 1819, for $15,000. Until August, 1865, this beautiful property remained intact— save that the trees ever grew larger and that the house took on a mellower tone as the years went on—and then it was swept away, and the existing stupid brick houses were built in its place.

For more than a century and a quarter the Warren house was the most important dwelling on this portion of the island. It was the nucleus about which other country-seats clustered—including, before the year 1767, those of William Bayard, James Jauncey, and Oliver De Lancey, Lady Warren's brother: whose estate, later, was confiscated because of his loyalty to the crown. Very proper and elegant people were all of these, and—their seats being at a convenient distance from the city—their elegant friends living in New York found pleasure in making Greenwich an objective point when taking the air of fine afternoons. And even when visiting was out of the question, a turn through Greenwich to the Monument was a favorite expedition among the gentlefolk of a century or so ago.

Until about the year 1767, access to this region was only by the Greenwich Road, close upon the line of the present Greenwich Street and directly upon the water-side. Where it crossed Lispenard's meadows (the low region lying on each side of the present Canal Street) and the marshy val-

ley (about Charlton Street) of the Manetta Creek,
the road was raised upon a causeway ; but not to
a sufficient height to save it from being heavy in
wet weather and in part under water with strong
spring tides. For the greater convenience of the
dwellers at Greenwich, therefore, inland communication between that region and the city was
provided for by opening a lane (formally ap-
proved in 1768) from the Post Road (now the
Bowery) westward across the fields. Two sections of this lane still are in existence: the bit
between the Bowery and Broadway (formerly Art
Street) that now is Astor Place ; and the bit between Eighth and Fourteenth streets that now is
Greenwich Avenue. Being prolonged more or
less on the lines thus established, the two sections
met near the northwest corner of the present
Washington Square.

Greenwich Lane was called also Monument
Lane and Obelisk Lane : for the reason that at
its northern extremity, a little north of the present Eighth Avenue and Fifteenth Street, was a
monument in honor of General Wolfe. After
the erection of this memorial to the hero of Que-
bec the drive of good society was out the Post
Road to the Greenwich turning ; thence across to
the Obelisk ; thence by the Great Kiln or Southampton Road (the present Gansevoort Street)
over to the Hudson ; and so homeward by the
river-side while the sun was sinking in golden
glory behind the Jersey hills. Or the drive could
be extended a little by going out the Post Road

as far as Love Lane, and thence south by the Southampton, Warren, or Fitzroy Road to the Great Kiln Road, and so by the water-side back to town.

With the exceptions noted, all of the old roads hereabouts have disappeared under the City Plan ; yet many traces of them still survive, and can be found by careful searching along their ancient lines.* For instance, the Union Road—which connected the Skinner and Great Kiln roads— seems at the first glance to have been entirely ploughed under. But such is not the case. It began about in the rear of the frame dwelling No. 33 West Eleventh Street ; and not two hundred feet from its beginning its slanting line across Twelfth Street still is defined clearly by the corner cut off and the corner projecting of the houses numbered 43 and 45. On West Thirteenth Street an old wooden house, No. 38, marks with its slanting side the line of the road ; and against this ancient structure has been erected within the present year (1894) a tall building, whereof the slanting eastern wall conforms to the road-line, covering in part the site of a still more picturesque wooden dwelling with outside stairs —built when all about here was open country— which was buried in the heart of the block.

As to the monument to General Wolfe, which

* In determining the lines of the old roads, and the boundaries of the old estates, I have had the assistance of Mr. Richard D. Cooke, the highest authority in such matters in New York, and the use of his unique collection of maps.

gave a name to Monument Lane and an objective point for afternoon drives, it seems to have
dissolved into thin air.  It certainly was in position during the British occupation of New York
in Revolutionary times, but since those times no
vestige of it has been found.  The theory has
been advanced that the English soldiers took
away with them this memorial of their gallant
countryman—fearing that harm might come to it
if left in a rebellious land.  But an obelisk is not
a handy thing for an army to carry around with
it, even though, as in this case, the obelisk is a
small one and the army is travelling by sea ; nor
is it so inconspicuous an object that it can be
picked up or set down by an army without attracting a certain amount of attention on the part
of the by-standers.  Therefore, I think that had
it really been put aboard ship, somebody here
would have chronicled the queer fact ; and that
had it been landed in another country, news as to
its whereabouts would have come to New York
in the century and more that has slipped away
since it disappeared.  On the other hand, had it
remained on this island, it ought still to be somewhere in sight.

On the line of the Monument Lane, or Greenwich Lane, lay the Potter's Field, a part of which
now is Washington Square.  In 1794 the Potter's
Field was established at the junction of the Post
Road and the Bloomingdale Road, on land now
a part of Madison Square ; but this site was abandoned three years later, partly because the United

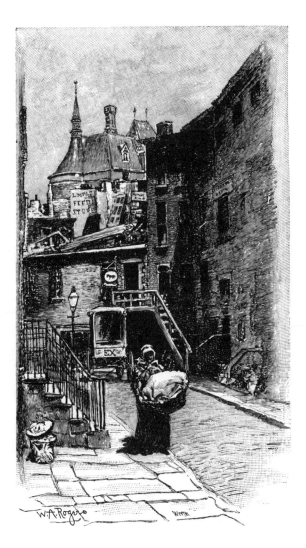

GAY STREET

States Arsenal was erected there, and partly because reasonable exception was taken to the ob-
trusion of pauper funerals upon the fashionable
drive.   On this latter score the move, in 1797, to
what is now Washington Square did not much
mend matters, and very strong remonstrances
were urged against it.   But the move was made,
and there the graveyard remained—on the north
side of the lane, about at the foot of the present
Fifth Avenue—until the year 1823.   It was not
strictly a pauper's graveyard—a fact that was
demonstrated by the unearthing of tombstones
(a luxury not accorded to paupers) while excavation was in progress, in the summer of 1890, for
the Washington Arch.   Much to my sorrow, I
was out of the country when these tombstones
were dug up; and, later, when I searched for
them, they had disappeared.

North of Greenwich Lane, extending from the
Bowery across to about the easterly line of the
present Fifth Avenue, was the Eliot estate; which
later was owned by Captain Robert Richard Randall, and was bequeathed by him (June 1, 1801)
for the founding of the Sailors' Snug Harbor.
The estate, in all, comprised about twenty-one
acres of good farming land; with which went the
mansion-house, and also two or three lots in the
First Ward.   It was Captain Randall's intention
that the Snug Harbor should be built upon this
property—for which he had paid £5000 when he
bought it, in 1790, from "Baron" Poelnitz—and
that the farm would supply all the grain and

vegetables which the inmates of the institution
would require. The trustees, however, perceived
that farming was not the most profitable use to
which the property could be put; and while the
suits to break the will still were pending, they
procured an act of the Legislature (April, 1828)
which enabled them to lease it and to purchase
the property on Staten Island where the asylum
now stands. But it was not until the year 1831,
the case having been settled definitely in favor of
the trust by the decision of the United States
Supreme Court in March, 1830, that this purchase
was made. At the time of Captain Randall's
death his estate yielded an annual income of
about $4000; by 1848 the income had increased
to nearly $40,000; by 1870 to a little more than
$100,000; and at the present time it is about
$350,000.

Valuable though the Snug Harbor property is,
it certainly would have increased in value far
more rapidly, and would be far more valuable as
a whole at the present day, had it fallen into the
market on its owner's death instead of becoming
leasehold property in perpetuity. Leaseholds are
the direct product of the law of entail or primo-
geniture—under which the title to land is held
only in trust by the male line in seniority, and
the fee becomes simple only when the line is
extinguished and a division made among the
general heirs. Holdings of this sort essentially
are un-American in principle, and have the practical inconvenience of two ownerships (which con-

NO. 260 WEST TENTH STREET

ceivably may become antagonistic) in what virtually is a single possession : a house, and the land on which it stands.

There is a very considerable amount of leasehold property in New York, and in almost every instance this encumbered land is less valuable—*i. e.*, brings in a smaller return—than land immediately adjoining it of which the fee may be transferred. In the case of the Snug Harbor estate the first leases, when the existing dwelling-houses were erected, were made to advantage ; but this tied-up property was skipped over, when business moved northward, in favor of the region above Fourteenth Street where the fee can be acquired

## V

Simultaneously with the founding of the country-seats at Greenwich, two small settlements of a humbler sort were formed on the shore of the North River in that region. One of these, known as Lower Greenwich, was at the foot of Brannan (now Spring) Street, and the other, known as Upper Greenwich, was at the foot of what now is Christopher Street and then was the Skinner Road. Of this latter an entire block still remains: the row of low wooden houses on West Street between Christopher and Tenth, of which the best view is from Wiehawken Street in the rear. These houses were standing, certainly, as far back as the year 1796—as is shown on the Commissioners' map by the indentation to accommodate them upon the State-prison property acquired in that year. Probably they are the houses indicated on the Ratzen Map as standing at this point one hundred and twenty-seven years ago.

The building of the State-prison brought to the upper village what might have been called— could the use of the word have been anticipated by four-fifths of a century—a boom. As passed, the act of Assembly of March 26, 1796, provided for the erection of two prisons, one in Albany and one in New York; but a subsequent modification of the act applied the entire sum appropriated—about $200,000—to the erection of a single

building here.   The prison stood at the foot of
Amos (now Tenth) Street, on the site occupied
by the existing brewery: into the structure of
which (as may be seen just inside the Tenth
Street entrance) have been incorporated parts of
the old walls.   The building—200 feet long, with
wings extending from it at right angles towards
the river—stood in grounds of about four acres in
extent; the whole enclosed by a stone-wall twen-

STATE PRISON

ty-two feet high on the side towards the river,
and fourteen feet high elsewhere.   One of my
aged gossips has told me that a wharf was built
out into the stream, but that it did not extend
far enough to be available at all stages of the
tide.   This particular gossip was a river-captain
in his day, sixty years and more ago, and among
the queer freights which he used to bring to the
city there would be now and then a load of convicts.   His passengers did not like it at all, he
said, when, the tide not serving, he was compelled

to carry them past the prison to which they were bound and to land them at the Battery: "and I must say I didn't wonder," he added. "Just think how it would be yourself—walkin' clost on to three mile of a br'ilin' summer day, with nothin' better'n gettin' jailed when you comed t' the end of it! It was only human natur' for them poor devils t' get up on their ears an' swear." Log rafts from up the river used to make fast near the State-prison wharf pending their purchase by the ship-builders and lumber-dealers down in the city. It was great fun, one of my cheery old gentlemen tells me, going in swimming off these rafts about sixty years ago.

The prison was opened November 28, 1797, when seventy prisoners were transferred thither, and it continued in use a little more than thirty years. The male prisoners were transferred to Sing Sing in 1828, and the female prisoners in the spring of 1829—when the entire property was sold into private hands. This was one of the first prisons in which convicts were taught trades; but for a long while the more conspicuous results of this benevolent system—a feature of which was the assembling together of the prisoners in large work-rooms, with consequent abundant oppor-tunities for concocting conspiracies—were dan-gerous plots and mutinous outbreaks. In June, 1799, fifty or sixty men revolted and seized their keepers; and not until the guards opened fire on them with ball cartridge—by which several were wounded, though none were killed—was the mutiny quelled.  In April, 1803, about forty men broke from the prison to the prison-yard, and, after setting fire to the building, attempted to scale the walls ; and again the guards came with their muskets and compelled order—this time killing as well as wounding—while the keepers put out the fire.  In May, 1804, a still more dangerous revolt occurred.  On this occasion the keepers were locked in the north wing of the building, which then was fired.  Fortunately, according to a contemporaneous account, "one more humane than the rest released the keepers" ; but the north wing was destroyed, involving a loss of $25,000, and in the confusion many of the prisoners escaped.  A long sigh of thankfulness must have gone up from Greenwich when this highly volcanic institution became a thing of the past.

Yet the people of Greenwich were disposed to feel a certain pride in their penal establishment, and to treat it as one of the attractions of their town—as appears from the following advertisement of the Greenwich Hotel in *The Columbian* of September 18, 1811 :

"A few gentlemen may be accommodated with board and lodging at this pleasant and healthy situation, a few doors from the State Prison.  The Greenwich stage passes from this to the Federal Hall and returns five times a day."

A little later, 1816, Asa Hall's line of stages was running : with departures from Greenwich on the even hours and from New York, at Pine

Street and Broadway, on the uneven hours all
day. The custom was to send to the stage office
to engage a seat to town; and then the stage
would call for the passenger, announcement being made of its approach—so that the passenger
might be ready and no time lost—by noble blasts
upon a horn. The fare each way was twenty-five
cents. One of the freshest and most delightful
of my old gentlemen remembers it all as clearly as though it were but yesterday—beginning
with his mother's brisk, " Now, Dan, run up to
Asa's and tell him to send the eight-o'clock
stage here"; continuing with a faint burst of
horn-blowing in the distance which grew louder
and louder until it stopped with a flourish at the
very door; and ending with the stage disappear-
ing, to the accompaniment of a gallant tooting
growing fainter and fainter, in a cloud of dust
down the country road.

This country road was the present Greenwich
Street south of Leroy. It was on Leroy Street
that my old gentleman lived, seventy years and
more ago, and all about his home were open
fields. Eastward the view was unobstructed
quite across to Washington Square — as he
knows positively because he remembers seeing
from his own front stoop the gallows which was
set up (near the present Washington Arch) for
the execution of one Rose Butler, a negro wench
who was hanged for murder in the year 1822.
(Another of my elderly acquaintances remembers
stealing away from home and going to this very

NO. 246 WEST TENTH STREET

hanging—and coming back so full of it that he could not keep his own secret, and so was most righteously and roundly spanked !)

South of Leroy Street was open country as far as Canal Street, "and probably farther"; but my gentleman is less certain, because there was no convenient gallows in that direction to fix a limit to his view. On this head, however, there is abundant evidence. Mr. Peter Gassner, treating of a period a little earlier—about the year 1803—writes: "Corri, another Frenchman, had a mead-garden and flying-horses on the eminence between Franklin and Leonard streets. It was at least fifty feet from [above] the road. You got to it by wooden stairs; and, when up, would overlook the space to Greenwich—nothing occupying the space until you met Borrowson's and old Tyler's, both mead-gardens and taverns." And the precise Mr. John Randel, Jun.—engineer to the Commissioners by whom was prepared, under the act of April 13, 1807, the present City Plan—writes that in the year 1809 he daily crossed the ditch at Canal Street on a wooden plank, and walked thence nearly the whole distance to Christopher Street through open fields.

The precise Mr. Randel recalls these facts in connection with a celebrity—perhaps I should say a notoriety—who lived in Greenwich at that period, and who died in the village on the 8th of June in the year just named. This was the author of *The Age of Reason*, Tom Paine. The

Commissioners at that time had their office at
the corner of Christopher and Herring (now
Bleecker) streets; and Paine, together with Madame Bonneville and her two sons, were lodged
in a house close by on Herring Street between
Christopher and Jones — a fortunate juxtaposi-
tion, since it caused Mr. Randel to leave behind
him this quaint record of his eminent infidel
neighbor: "I boarded in the city," he writes,
"and in going to the office I almost daily passed
the house in Herring Street (now 293 Bleecker)
where Thomas Paine resided, and frequently in
fair weather saw him sitting at the south window
of the first-story room of that house. The sash
was raised, and a small table or stand was placed
before him with an open book placed upon it
which he appeared to be reading. He had his
spectacles on, his left elbow rested upon the table or stand, and his chin rested between the
thumb and fingers of his hand; his right hand
lay upon his book, and a decanter containing liq-
uor of the color of rum or brandy was standing
next his book or beyond it. I never saw Thomas
Paine at any other place or in any other position."

In the last month of Paine's life, in order to
make him more comfortable than was possible
in a lodging-house, Madame Bonneville hired a
small frame dwelling — standing deep in the
block, and but a stone's-throw from that in
which they then were living—and removed him
thither. The main building of this house stood

WIEHAWKEN STREET

on land that now is a part of Grove Street. The street was opened shortly after Paine's death (having first the name of Cozine; later, Columbia; still later, Burrows; and, finally, Grove), and then was deflected out of line so as to leave the house standing. In the year 1836 the street was widened and straightened, and then the whole of the main building was destroyed. The back building, in which Paine died, remained until a much later period; and then was replaced by the present brick dwelling, No. 59. The present Barrow Street—running parallel with Grove, and opened between Herring (Bleecker) and Asylum (West Fourth) about the same time—was known for a time as Raisin Street; and this name was a corruption of Reason Street—given to it by the Commissioners in compliment to the author of *Common Sense*, who was their near neighbor in Greenwich Village for more than a year.

It was during Paine's last days in the little house in Greenwich that two worthy divines, the Rev. Mr. Milledollar and the Rev. Mr. Cunningham, sought to bring him to a realizing sense of the error of his ways. Their visitation was not a success. "Don't let 'em come here again," he said, curtly, to his house-keeper, Mrs. Hedden, when they had departed; and added: "They trouble me." In pursuance of this order, when they returned to the attack, Mrs. Hedden denied them admission—saying with a good deal of piety, and with even more common - sense: "If

God does not change his mind, I'm sure no human can!" And so this sturdy sceptic was left
to die peacefully in his unfaith.


VI

What tended most to develop Greenwich into
a town—a cause more potent than its embryotic
trade in lumber, its very small ferry, and its ex-
plosive prison, all combined — was its positive
healthfulness; and the consequent security which
it offered to refugees from the city when pestilence was abroad. The salubrity of this region
(which is as marked now, relatively, as it was a
century ago) is due to its excellent natural drainage, and to the fact that its underlying soil to a
depth of at least fifty feet is a pure sand. In
former times the sanitary conditions were still
more favorable — when the ample space about
the scattered houses assured an abundance of
fresh air, and when the stretch of more than a
mile of open country between the village and the
city constituted a barrier which no pestilence but
small-pox ever overcame.

It is in connection with small-pox that I find
the first reference to Greenwich as a place of refuge. This occurs in a letter dated April 18, 1739,
from Lieutenant-Governor Clarke to the Duke of
Newcastle, beginning: " I beg leave to inform
your Grace that, the Small Pox being in town,
and one third part of the Assembly not having

NO. 135 WASHINGTON PLACE

had it, I gave them leave to sit at Greenwich, a
small village about two or three miles out of
town." In this case, however, safety was not se-
cured—for "the Small Pox" went along with the
Assemblymen to Greenwich and sat there too.

It is hard to realize nowadays the deadliness
of those early times in New York—before small-
pox was controlled by vaccination and before yellow-fever was guarded against by a tolerably effective system of quarantine. Judging from the

newspaper references to it, small-pox seems to
have been a regular feature of every winter;
while yellow-fever was so frequent a visitor that
Mr. John Lambert, in his sketch of New York in
the year 1807, wrote : " The malignant, or yellow, fever generally commences in the confined
parts of the town, near the water-side, in the
month of August or September." And to this,
still in the same matter-of-course manner, Mr.
Lambert added : " As soon as this dreadful
scourge makes its appearance in New York the
inhabitants shut up their shops and fly from
their houses into the country. Those who cannot go far, on account of business, remove to
Greenwich, a small village situate on the border
of the Hudson River about two or three miles
from town. Here the merchants and others have
their offices, and carry on their concerns with little danger from the fever, which does not seem
to be contagious beyond a certain distance. The
banks and other public offices also remove their
business to this place ; and markets are regularly
established for the supply of the inhabitants.
Very few are left in the confined parts of the
town except the poorer classes and the negroes.
The latter, not being affected by the fever, are of
great service at that dreadful crisis ; and are the
only persons who can be found to discharge the
hazardous duties of attending the sick and burying the dead. Upward of 20,000 people removed from the interior parts of the city and
from the streets near the water-side in 1805."

A WINTER NIGHT IN GROVE STREET

Yellow-fever seems to have been epidemic for the first time in New York in the summer of 1703. It was not recognized as yellow-fever, and is referred to in the records of the time as " the great sickness "; but from the description given of it, coupled with the fact that the infection was traced to a ship come in from St. Thomas, there is little room for doubt in regard to the nature of the disease. The mortality was so considerable that a panic seized upon the inhabitants of the city, and they fled to the country for safety— thus establishing the habit to which Mr. Lambert refers as being fixed so firmly a century later on. Again, in the summers of 1742 and 1743 there was " a malignant epidemic strongly resembling the yellow-fever in type," which caused upward of two hundred deaths in the latter year.

But the most severe fever summers of the last century came close together in its final decade. Of these the first was 1791, in which the death-rate was comparatively low; the second, 1795, was more severe, the deaths rising to upward of seven hundred; while in the course of the third, 1798 (when more than two thousand deaths occurred, and the city was forsaken by its inhabitants and commerce for a time was crushed), the fever became an overwhelming calamity. While the panic lasted, not only Greenwich but all the towns and villages roundabout were crowded with refugees.

The epidemics of fever which appeared with great frequency during the first quarter of the

present century culminated in the direful summer
of 1822—when, under stress of the worst panic
ever caused by fever in this city, the town fairly
exploded and went flying beyond its borders as
though the pestilence had been a bursting mine.
Hardie gives the following vivid sketch of the
exodus: "Saturday, the 24th August, our city
presented the appearance of a town besieged.
From daybreak till night one line of carts, containing boxes, merchandise, and effects, were seen
moving towards Greenwich Village and the upper
parts of the city. Carriages and hacks, wagons
and horsemen, were scouring the streets and filling the roads; persons with anxiety strongly
marked on their countenances, and with hurried
gait, were hustling through the streets. Temporary stores and offices were erecting, and even
on the ensuing day (Sunday) carts were in mo-
tion, and the saw and hammer busily at work.
Within a few days thereafter the Custom-house,
the Post-office, the banks, the insurance offices,
and the printers of newspapers located themselves
in the village or in the upper part of Broadway,
where they were free from the impending danger;
and these places almost instantaneously became
the seat of the immense business usually carried
on in the great metropolis."

Devoe, who quotes the above in his *Market
Book*, adds: "The visits of yellow-fever in 1798,
'99, 1803, and '5, tended much to increase the formation of a village near the Spring Street Market
and one also near the State Prison ; but the fever

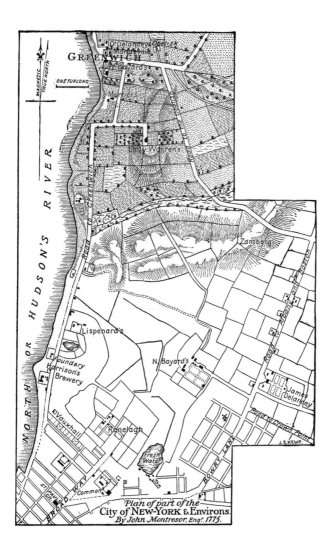

Plan of part of the
City of NEW-YORK & Environs.
By John Montresor, Engr. 1775.

of 1822 built up many streets with numerous
wooden buildings for the uses of the merchants,
banks (from which Bank Street took its name),
offices, etc.; and the celerity of putting up these
buildings is better told by the Rev'd Mr. Mar-
selus, who informed me that he saw corn growing on the present corner of Hammond [West
Eleventh] and Fourth streets on a Saturday
morning, and on the following Monday Sykes &
Niblo had a house erected capable of accommo-
dating three hundred boarders. Even the Brooklyn ferry-boats ran up here daily."

Among the more notable of the remnants of
the time when the Greenwich region for the most
part was open country are those at the southeast
corner of Eleventh Street and the Sixth Avenue:
the little triangular graveyard and the two old
framed dwellings which now rest on the lines of
the street and the avenue, but which primitively
stood — a few feet from their present site — on
the now almost obliterated Milligan's Lane.

The triangular graveyard is a remnant of the
second Beth Haim, or Place of Rest, owned on
this island by the Jews. The first Beth Haim—
purchased in 1681 and enlarged in 1729—is on
the line of the elevated railway just south of
Chatham Square. This was closed early in the
present century, and then the Beth Haim at
Greenwich was purchased—a plot of ground with
a front of about fifty feet on Milligan's Lane, and
thence extending, a little east of south, about one
hundred and ten feet. In the year 1830, when

Eleventh Street was opened on the lines of the City Plan—saving only the bit between Broadway and the Bowery, on which stood the house of the stiff-necked Mr. Henry Brevoort—almost the whole of the Jewish burial-ground was swept away. The street went directly across it—leaving only the corner on its south side, and a still smaller corner on its north side.

## VII

Greenwich Village always has been to me the most attractive portion of New York. It has the positive individuality, the age, much of the picturesqueness, of that fascinating region of which the centre is Chatham Square; yet it is agreeably free from the foul odors and the foul humanity which make expeditions in the vicinity of Chatham Square, while abstractly delightful, so stingingly distressing to one's nose and soul.

Greenwich owes its picturesqueness to the protecting spirit of grace which has saved its streets from being rectangular and its houses from being all alike; and which also has preserved its many quaintnesses and beauties of age—with such resulting blessings as the view around the curve in Grove Street towards St. Luke's Church, or under the arch of trees where Grove and Christopher streets are mitred together by the little park, and the many friendly old houses which stand squarely on their right to be individual and have their own opinion of the rows of modern dwellings all made of precisely the same material cast in precisely the same mould.

The cleanliness, moral and physical, of the village is accounted for by the fact that from the very beginning it has been inhabited by a humanity of the better sort. From Fourteenth Street down to Canal Street, west of the meridian of the Sixth Avenue, distinctively is the American quarter of New York. A sprinkling of French and Italians is found within these limits, together with the few Irish required for political purposes; and in the vicinity of Carmine Street are scattered some of the tents of the children of Ham. But with these exceptions the population is composed of substantial, well-to-do Americans—and it really does one's heart good, on the Fourth of July and the 22d of February, to see the way the owners of the roomy, comfortable houses which here abound proclaim their nationality by setting the trim streets of Greenwich gallantly ablaze with American flags. As compared with the corresponding region on the east side — where a score of families may be found packed into a single building, and where even the bad smells have foreign names—this American quarter of New York is a liberal lesson in cleanliness, good citizenship, and self-respect.

And how interesting are the people whom one hereabouts encounters (with but the most trifling effort of the imagination) stepping along the ancient thoroughfares which once knew them in ma-

HOME FOR AGED COUPLES, HUDSON STREET, OPPOSITE GROVE

terial form !—Wouter Van Twiller, chuckling over
his easily won tobacco plantation ; the Labadist
envoys, rejoicing because of their discovery of a
country permissive of liberty of conscience and
productive of good beer ; General Ol. De Lancey—wearing the Tory uniform which later cost
him his patrimony—taking the air with his sister,
Lady Warren, the stout, bewigged Sir Peter, and
the three little girls ; Governor Clinton, with the
harried look of one upon whom an advance-copy
of the Declaration of Independence has been
served ; Senator Richard Henry Lee, of Virginia,
who honored Greenwich by making it his home
during the session of Congress in 1789 ; Master
Tom Paine—escaped from Madame Bonneville
and the little boys in the house in Grove Street
—on his way to the Old Grapevine for a fresh
jug of rum ; Friend Jacob Barker, looking with
satisfaction at the house in Jane Street bought
by the butcher who had enough faith in the
shrewd old Quaker to take the doubtful notes of
his bank at par. Only in Greenwich, or below
the City Hall—a region over-noisy for wraiths—
will one meet agreeable spectres such as these.

# DOWN LOVE LANE

## I

AS all the world knows — barring, of course,
that small portion of the world which is not
familiar with old New York—the Kissing Bridge
of a century ago was on the line of the Boston
Post Road (almost precisely at the intersection
of the Third Avenue and Seventy-seventh Street
of the present day), about four miles out of town.
And all the world, without any exception whatever, must know that after crossing a kissing-
bridge the ridiculously short distance of four
miles is no distance at all. Fortunately for the
lovers of that period, it was possible to go roundabout from the Kissing Bridge to New York by
a route which very agreeably prolonged the oscupontine situation : that is to say, by the Abingdon
Road, close on the line of the present Twenty-
first Street, to the Fitzroy Road, nearly parallel from Fifteenth Street to Forty-second Street
with the present Eighth Avenue ; thence down
to the Great Kiln Road, on the line of the present Gansevoort Street ; thence to the Greenwich
Road, on the line of the present Greenwich Street
—and so, along the river-side, comfortably slowly
back to town.

It is a theory of my own that the Abingdon Road received a more romantic name because it was the first section of this devious departure from the strait path leading townward into the broad way which certainly led quite around Robin Hood's barn, and may also have led to destruction, but which bloomed with the potentiality of a great many extra kisses wherewith the Kissing Bridge (save as a point of departure) had nothing in the world to do. I do not insist upon my theory, but I state as an undeniable fact that in the latter half of the last century the Abingdon Road was known generally—and, I infer from contemporary allusions to it, favorably—as Love Lane.

To avoid confusion, and also to show how necessary were such amatory appurtenances to the gentle-natured inhabitants of this island in earlier times, I must here state that the primitive Kissing Bridge was in that section of the Post Road which now is Chatham Street; and that in this same vicinity—on the Rutgers estate—was the primitive Love Lane. It was of the older institution that an astute and observant traveller in this country, the Rev. Mr. Burnaby, wrote in his journal a century and a half ago: "Just before you enter the town there is a little bridge, commonly called 'the kissing-bridge,' where it is customary, before passing beyond, to salute the lady who is your companion"—to which custom the reverend gentleman seems to have taken with a very tolerable relish, and to have found "curious, yet not displeasing."

The later Love Lane, the one with which I am
now concerned, was but little travelled—being,
primarily, the approach from the highway to
Captain Clarke's estate known as Chelsea—and
for a good many years lovers had the chief use
of it ; yet was it used also a little by polite society taking the air of fine summer afternoons : up
the Bloomingdale Road to this turning, thence
across to the river-side, and so homeward to New
York, being one of the longest of the ordinary afternoon drives.

To the south of the lane lay the estate—extending from the present Broadway to the present Eighth Avenue—that was presented by the
Corporation to Captain Warren, afterwards Admiral Sir Peter Warren, in the year 1745, in
grateful recognition, ostensibly, of his capture of
Louisburg ; but really, I fancy, because a good
many of the leading citizens were under obliga-
tions to him of one sort or another for benefits
derived from the many prizes which he had sent
into this port to be condemned.    Later, when
the whole of the Warren estate was partitioned,
two roads were opened out from the Abingdon
Road across this northern portion of the property.    The first of these, known as the Southampton Road (Sir Peter's second daughter, Ann,
married Charles Fitzroy, who later became the
Baron of Southampton : his eldest daughter,
Charlotte, married the Earl of Abingdon), was a
continuation of the Great Kiln Road from—to
use existing designations—the Seventh Avenue

and Fifteenth Street to Eighteenth Street just
east of the Sixth Avenue, and thence parallel
with the Sixth Avenue to the northern side of
Twenty-first Street. The second, known as the
Warren Road, left the Southampton Road at
Sixteenth Street and ran parallel with, and a lit-
tle to the east of, the Seventh Avenue, also to
Twenty-first Street.

At Twenty-first Street and Broadway there is
nothing now to suggest that ever a Love Lane
was thereabouts; and the Fifth Avenue crossing
of Twenty-first Street—with a huge nine-story
building on one side and the traditionally respectable Union Club on the other—presents so
forbidding an appearance that the searcher after
traces of these old-time by-ways well may be
induced to abandon at the very outset, all un-
timely, his gentle quest. But he who hunts for
ancient landmarks must not be discouraged easily; and this particular hunt, in the happy end,
reveals so astonishingly large a survival that the
sadness of the beginning is swept away and lost
in a flood of genuine antiquarian joy. The fact,
indeed, really is extraordinary that this part of
the city—which has the appearance to the ordinary observer of being essentially modern and
uninteresting—should so teem with signs and
relics of a truly interesting past.

## II

The first traces of the Abingdon Road, otherwise Love Lane, found in West Twenty-first
Street are the little two-story brick houses, Nos.
25, 27, which stand back from the street and af-
fect a rural and cottage-like air on an insufficient
capital of narrow veranda. These houses certainly were built after the present City Plan had
been adopted (1811); and probably were built
not much more than forty years ago—a little after the creation of London Terrace had sent into
this bit of country-side a premature thrill of speculative activity. Yet while thus essentially modern, they cling affectionately—using their meagre
verandas and village-like front yards as tentacles
—to the traditions of a really rural past.

Only a little farther westward is a row of three
houses, Nos. 51, 53, 55, which very obviously be-
long to the period to which the others only aspire.
They are built of brick, are very small, and are
only two stories and a half high : and seem still
lower because the grade of the present street actually is two or three inches above the level of the
ground-floor. Even yet in the rear of the little
houses are deep gardens in which are genuine
vines and, as a theatrical person would style
them, practicable trees. They are the delight,
these gardens, of the present French inhabitants
of the tiny dwellings: as any passer-by about

A CHELSEA DOORWAY

noon-time of a fine summer's day may see for himself, with no more trouble than is involved in looking through one of the open front doors, down a tunnel-like passage, to the sunny open space in the rear — where he will behold (surrounded by conspicuous evidences of clear-starching) a gay Gallic company breakfasting under its own vine and ailantus-tree with such honest lightheartedness as can be manifested only by French folk eating something—eating almost anything— out-of-doors.

At first these houses were a bit of a mystery to me. I could not understand why, especially, they should be just there. But a reference to the Commissioners' map explained that they had been built upon what once was an eligible corner lot— at the very point, in fact, where the Southampton Road came into Love Lane. It has occurred to me that the three little houses may have been, originally, a single house which served as a roadside tavern. Here would have been almost precisely the half-way point in the long drive out from town and back again of an afternoon; and at this particular corner—the Southampton Road being a short-cut down to Greenwich and across to the Great Kiln Road—would have been intercepted the whole procession of thirsty wayfarers. Possibly, the tavern prospering, the tavern-keeper may have built out of his profits the large house, with quaint windows in the gable of its weatherboarded side, which still stands at the northeast corner of Twenty-first Street and the Sixth Ave-

nue; and thereto may have retired, when sufficiently enriched by his genial trade, to spend in
luxurious idleness the Indian summer of his alco-
holic days.

West of the Sixth Avenue is a large open space
which testifies silently yet strongly to the time
when all this part of the island was quiet country-
side and the city still was very far away. It is
the Jewish graveyard — the Beth Haim, or Place
of Rest. Sixty years and more ago the Beth
Haim at Greenwich was swept away (save the
little corner which still remains east of the Sixth
Avenue) by the opening of Eleventh Street.
Then it was that the Beth Haim was established here — on a lot which possessed the advantages of lying within one of the blocks of the
new City Plan, and therefore was safe against
the opening of new streets, and which also could
be reached by an already opened country road.
Although long since superseded by the Beth
Haim on Long Island, this graveyard still is
cared for zealously—as may be seen by looking
from the back windows of the big dry-goods
shop on the Sixth Avenue upon its rows of
seemly monuments, whereon are legends in He-
brew characters telling of " Rest " and " Peace."
And, truly, looking out from the bustle and
clamor of the shop upon the grassy quiet place,
with its ivy clad dead-house and its long lines
of marble gravestones whereof the whiteness
has become gray as the years have gone on and
on, there is a most pleasant sense of rest and

S. W. CORNER OF EIGHTH AVENUE AND TWENTY-SECOND STREET

peacefulness amid this calm serenity of ancient death.

Save for the graveyard, there is no sign—at least, I have not found any sign — between the Sixth and Seventh avenues of the old country road. In this block Love Lane seems to have been ploughed under completely. The houses on both sides of the street, having still about them an air of decayed smugness, date from the period, thirty years or so ago, when West Twenty-third Street was pluming itself (vastly to the amusement of Second Avenue and Gramercy Park and Stuyvesant and Washington squares) upon being quite the smartest street of the town; and when Twenty-first and Twenty-second streets, catching a little reflected glory from this near-by glitter of fashion, exalted their horns above horns in general and gave audible thanks that they were not at all as were the other streets over on that part of the West Side. It is not surprising, therefore, that from this section of Twenty-first Street the modest memory of Love Lane should have disappeared.

The trail shows again in the middle of the next block, between the Seventh and Eighth avenues, in the little houses standing far back from the present street in deep yards. But the most conspicuous house in the block—the large dwelling standing in its own grounds and having so quaint and so agreeably dignified an air that one instantly is disposed to classify it as a survival from the beginning of the present century—is not an antique at all.  Actually, it was built but twenty-five or thirty years ago; and its owner, being a boss-mason—the builder of the Fourth Avenue tunnel—built it for himself according to his own notions and in his own way.  Though a large house, it is not at all a grand one; but there is not a house in New York that excels it in the matter of positive individuality.  It is delightful to see how much meaning and character its builder contrived to put into it while yet employing only simple means.  He is dead, this excellent boss-mason; but in the long stable beside the mansion-house still is preserved his original kit of mason's tools.  Never in his lifetime would he permit them to be disturbed, and his wishes concerning them have survived his death.

For many years the Abingdon Road—to give it at parting its more dignified name—ended at the line where now is the Eighth Avenue and where then was the Fitzroy Road.  Later, certainly before the year 1811, it was carried westward to the shore of the Hudson.  But the weather-boarded, hip-roofed house still extant on the southwestern corner of this ancient crossway is to be classed less as a survival of Love Lane than of Chelsea Village: that ambitious suburb which, sixty years or so ago, made its somewhat premature start in life on the lines of the City Plan.

A SIDE GATE IN CHELSEA

## III

"Dead as Chelsea!" is a phrase which has been current in the British army since the battle of Fontenoy — when a British grenadier, of unknown name but epigrammatic habit, first used it in apostrophizing himself when a round-shot took off his right leg, and so gave him his billet to the Royal Hospital. That he rammed an oath down on top of this observation was no more than natural. A military authority of the highest—the late Captain Shandy, of Leven's regiment of Foot, who served in those very parts but a half-century earlier—has left on record his testimony to the exceeding profanity of the British troops in the Low Countries.

Almost contemporaneously with this lasting utterance of the Fontenoy grenadier, an American soldier, Captain Thomas Clarke, a veteran officer of the Provincial service who had done some very pretty fighting in the old French war, gave the name of Chelsea to his country-seat—a modest estate on the shores of the Hudson, between two and three miles north of the town of New York. And he chose this name, he said, because the home to which he gave it was to be the retreat of an old soldier in the evening of his days. So nice a touch was there of the fanciful and the poetic in the selection of such a name at a period—'twas in the year 1750—when neither poetry nor fancy had become rooted in American soil, that one's heart warms towards this gentle warrior in the certainty that he must have possessed a subtler and a finer nature than fell to the lot of most men of his country and his time.

There is yet another touch of pathos in the fact that the Captain, after all, did not die in this retreat which he had hoped would shelter him until the end. While his last illness was upon him his home was burned to the ground, and he himself was but barely saved from burning with it by rescuing neighbors, who carried him to a near-by farm-house—where he and Death came presently to terms.

When all was over, Mistress Molly Clarke, the Captain's widow, being a capable and energetic woman still in her prime, set herself to the work of rebuilding ; and found, no doubt, some measure of comfort and solace in being thus busily employed. The house then built was a large square structure of two stories, standing upon the crest of a little hill which sloped gently to the river-side, a hundred yards or so away. In relation to the present City Plan, the house stood two hundred feet or thereabouts west of the present Ninth Avenue, with its northern corner on the southern line of Twenty-third Street.

Mistress Molly, I fancy, had a fair allowance of peppery energy. When the Revolutionary war came on she had the pluck to remain—with her two pretty daughters—in her country-house, although the house was at no great distance from

THE MOORE HOUSE

the American fortified camp. To her sore vexation, a squad of Continentals was billeted upon her; and her distress was so reasonable that the officer in command — who, likely enough, had daughters of his own at home, and so was tenderly considerate of her proper motherly alarm — made a report of the matter to the commanding general. A good deal was going on just then to engross this general's attention; but, being a Virginian and a gentleman, he found time to ride over to Chelsea — on that famous white horse which curvets so dashingly in the background of Trumbull's picture — that he might express to Madam Clarke his regret that she had been troubled, and at the same time assure her that her trouble was at an end. Truly, it was very handsomely done!

While the American forces still were in possession of the island, and before the billet on
Chelsea had been withdrawn, an English frigate
stood up the river one day to give her crew
practical exercise at the guns, and in the course
of her firing pitched a shot fairly into Mrs.
Clarke's dwelling; which shot hurt nobody, but
made necessary some patch - work carpentering
that ever afterwards showed where the ball had
come cracking along. Mistress Molly happened
to be abroad when this bit of military incivility
occurred; and her first news of it was from one
of her billet of soldiers whom she met as she
was driving home, and who hailed her briskly
with the announcement: " The British have fired
a shot into your house, Mrs. Clarke !" To which
her ladyship replied instantly, and with a not
unreasonable bitterness: " Thank *you* for that !"
and so drove homeward in a fine temper in her
chaise.

Mistress Molly was near half a century behind her Captain in the eternal march. She died
in the year 1802. At her death the dwelling,
together with a part of the estate, passed to
Bishop Moore and his wife; and by them, in the
year 1813, was conveyed to the late Clement C.
Moore, their son. Upon coming into possession
of this last-named gentleman another story was
added to the house, and cellars were dug beneath the old foundation : in which reconstruct-
ed form the mansion remained standing—within
its terraced and beautiful grounds, at a consider-

able elevation above the street level—until about forty years ago. Possibly this old house was more picturesque than it was comfortable. Certainly its owner did not seem greatly to regret its loss. To his brief history of the property, from which the facts given above are extracted, he added the curt statement that when "the corporation of the city ordered a bulkhead to be built along the river-front it was thought advisable, if not absolutely necessary, to dig down the whole place and throw it into the river; when, of course, the old house was destroyed."

IV

It was to Mr. Clement C. Moore that Chelsea owed its existence as a village a long while in advance of the period when it became a part of the city of New York. His estate, by inheritance and by purchase, extended from the north side of the present Nineteenth Street to the south side of the present Twenty-fourth Street, and from the west side of the present Eighth Avenue to the river. Sixty years or so ago he began opening through his property the existing streets and avenues on the lines of the City Plan; and thereafter he gave his energies to founding and to fostering his town — to which access from New York was easy, either by way of Love Lane from the Bloomingdale Road, or by either of the roads from New York to Greenwich and thence

by the Fitzroy Road for the final three-quarters
of a mile.

The most notable dwellings erected in that
early time were those which comprise the still
existing rows on Twenty-third and Twenty-fourth
streets : London Terrace and Chelsea Cottages,
as they respectively were, and continue to be,
called. The first of these is the row, between
the Ninth and Tenth avenues, of tall pilastered
houses which gives one the impression of an Institution not very firmly fixed in its own mind
and liable to become something else, yet having
an air both gracious and friendly because of its
deep gardens and many tall old trees ; and the
second is in part a reproduction of the pilastered
houses upon a smaller scale, and in part chunky
little two-story houses with little pudgy bay-
windows and with ornate little porches over their
little doors. All of these dwellings, small and
large, are at odds with their present city surroundings because of their affectation of a countrified
air ; yet must they have been far more at odds
with their surroundings when they were erected
—being then remote in the country, yet pre-
sumptuously aping the manners of the town.

Both terrace and cottages date from almost
half a century ago. The block on which they
stand was leased by Mr. Moore to William Torrey on May 1, 1845 ; and Torrey thereafter built
and sold the houses subject to the lease — the
owner of the estate wisely retaining the fee. To
a slightly more remote period belongs the large

CHELSEA SQUARE—THE WEST BUILDING

square brick house on the Ninth Avenue, between Twentieth and Twenty-first streets; a house so citylike that passing strangers must have regarded it as some trick in optics when first it sprang up in that open country-side near sixty years ago. And now, the city pressing close around it, it also has somewhat of a country air: yet this is due mainly to the ample reaches of land about it—a lawn with a tennis-court at one side, and a sweet-smelling old-fashioned garden in the rear.

These conspicuous features of what once was Chelsea Village assert themselves—not offensively, yet with insistence born of a proper respect for their own dignity—upon the merest loiterer through the ancient roadways of the little town; and even a few of the more modest remnants of that earlier period, the little wooden houses wherein dwelt folk of a humbler sort, still may be seen here and there: standing back shyly from the street in deep yards, and having somewhat the abashed look of aged rustics confronted suddenly with city ways. But many more of these timber-toed veterans—true Chelsea pensioners—lie hidden away in the centres of the blocks, and may be found only by burrowing through alleyways beneath the outer line of prim brick houses of a modern time. Notably, on both sides of Twentieth Street, between the Seventh and Eighth avenues, these inner rows of houses may be found; and west of the Eighth Avenue on the northern side of the way. But one may rest as-

sured that wherever, in any of the blocks hereabouts, an alleyway opens there will be found an
old wooden house or a whole row of old wooden
houses at its inner end.

Geographically, and in all other ways, the central feature of Chelsea — from before its ambi-
tiously early essay at being a village on its own
account even until this present day when it is
in the city but not exactly of it—is the General
Theological Seminary of the Protestant Episco-
pal Church. To this institution was given rent
free by Clement C. Moore—the good Bishop, his
father, no doubt having a share in the prompting
of the gift — the whole of the block between
Twentieth and Twenty-first streets and the Ninth
and Tenth avenues; which lot, being for many
years only in small part built upon, long was
known as Chelsea Square. Here was laid the
corner-stone of the East Building of the Seminary on the 28th of July, 1825; and of the West
Building ten years later — both structures, with
the minor edifices erected later, being of a dark
gray stone which made an admirable color com-
position with the green of the grass and trees,
and of the ivy when it began to grow later on.
Only one of the original edifices, the West Building, still is standing; and now the larger part of
what was Chelsea Square is covered with the
great brick halls, and the brick chapel, erected
within the past ten years.

Even with all this growth of new buildings
there still remains a wide extent of trimly kept

CHELSEA SQUARE—MODERN COLLEGE BUILDINGS

lawns dotted with flower-beds and shaded by wide-branching trees; and there is no more delightful bit in all New York than the deeply recessed space in the south front, where the yellow-green lawn has for background the ivy-clad red brick walls of the chapel, far above which rises stately the gravely graceful square brick tower. Especially pleasing and Old-Worldly is this same place of a bright spring afternoon during the last five minutes' ringing of the chapel bell — when the seemly young Seminarists (every one of whom reasonably may hope to be a bishop before he dies) come trooping along the paths or across the grass to the chapel entrance, all properly clad in caps and gowns; while at the same time come up the pathway from the street to that same entrance (for their souls' comforting) some of the most charming and most charmingly dressed young gentlewomen to be found within a radius of a mile around. Truly, looking at this pretty sight, it is not difficult to fancy one's self a whole Atlantic away from New York in one of the English university towns.

Just across the Ninth Avenue, eastward from the Seminary, on Twentieth Street, is another picturesque bit: St. Peter's Church — a large structure of dark gray stone with a tall and massive and very well proportioned tower. Seen in broad daylight, the church is a good deal the worse for its Perpendicular porch built of pine planks, and for its absurd wooden crenellation. But these incongruous qualities disappear when dusk is falling; and in moonlight they become glorified into realities instead of cheap shams. At such times this church is beautiful with a grave beauty that fitly is its own.

CHELSEA COTTAGES, ON TWENTY-FOURTH STREET

The Fitzroy Road, leading from Greenwich to Chelsea and thence onward to the Bloomingdale Road, was closed as the streets of the City Plan were opened; but it has by no means disappeared. It may be traced more or less clearly from its beginning, south of Fifteenth Street, to its ending, at Forty-second Street: being throughout its entire length close upon the Eighth Avenue line. Principally is its former course marked—and this is true of all the old roads hereabouts—by open spaces in the rows of houses, or by houses of only a story or two stories in height, and usually of wood: as though some doubt as to the title to land which for so long a period had been surrendered to the public use had prevented the building upon it of anything, or had prompted the building of houses of small cost. These signs are not certain. At Twentieth, Nineteenth, and Sixteenth streets there are no traces of the road at all. On the other streets south of Twenty-first its crossing is clearly marked. At Twentieth Street it passed through the opening yet remaining between the wooden houses Nos. 250, 252; at Eighteenth Street an actual section of it remains in use in the driveway to a brewery; at Seventeenth Street another section remains, west of the wooden house No. 246, in the court running into the centre of the block; at Fifteenth Street it passed,

A TENNIS-COURT IN CHELSEA

beside the old gambrel-roofed house still standing, across the space now occupied by the one-story buildings Nos. 231, 233. Its union with the Great Kiln Road was made a little south of the present Fifteenth Street, in the heart of the existing block; the Fifteenth Street crossing, therefore, virtually is its southern end.

There was also, I am inclined to believe—although it is not marked on the Commissioners'

map—a road which ran parallel with the Fitzroy
Road a little east of the present Ninth Avenue.
What I take to be a trace of it on Twenty-first
Street is the two-story stable, No. 341, beside a
large frame house; on Twentieth and Nineteenth
streets no sign of it appears; on Eighteenth Street
the one-story shop, No. 368, seems to be another
trace; on Seventeenth Street, between the wood-
en houses Nos. 352, 354, there still is a driveway
into the middle of the block, where more wooden
houses of ancient date are found; on Sixteenth
Street the trace is a modern two-story dwelling,
No. 352, in the rear of which is a small wooden
house with old-fashioned outside stair; and on
Fifteenth Street the traces are the one-story
buildings on each side of the way, Nos. 366, 367;
on Fourteenth Street, naturally, no trace survives,
for here it would have merged into the Great
Kills Road.

But the most substantial evidence in favor of
this vanished and unrecorded roadway is found
in the two delightfully picturesque old wooden
houses which stand in the rear of No. 112 Ninth
Avenue—up an alluring alley and in a little court
of their own. They are of the same type as those
on Eighteenth Street of which a picture is given
on page 188, but the outside stairs leading to the
second story are not roofed over. Houses of this
sort were common in New York half a century
and more ago, and many of them, hidden away
inside the blocks as these are, still survive. They
possessed the very positive merit of giving the

privacy of an entirely separate dwelling to the tenants of each floor. These houses, in the rear of No. 112, certainly were built long before the Ninth Avenue was opened, and must have faced directly upon the old road; in additional proof of which conjecture is the fact that they stand precisely in line with the opening on Eighteenth Street where the road presumably crossed. Possibly the road never was opened officially. It may have been only a short-cut from the end of the Greenwich Road (of which, another point in its favor, it would have been a direct continuation) to Chelsea across the fields.

Of the Warren Road there is no trace on either Twenty-first or Twentieth Street; but its track is marked on Nineteenth Street by the wooden house No. 148; on Eighteenth Street by the houses Nos. 155, 157; and on Seventeenth Street by the house No. 154.

VI

Of all these old roads the Southampton was the most thickly settled, and has left behind it the strongest surviving traces. Excepting Twentieth Street, there is not one of the modern streets throughout its length but exhibits distinct marks of its ancient course; while the line of the Great Kiln Road, of which it was a continuation, is shown clearly by the oblique side wall of the house at the northwest corner of Fifteenth Street

THE CHAPEL DOOR, CHELSEA SQUARE

and the Seventh Avenue. Its most marked and most interesting remnant, however, is the group of wooden houses—buried in the heart of the block between Sixteenth and Seventeenth streets and the Sixth and Seventh avenues—built seventy years back, and long known as Paisley Place, or "the Weavers' Row."

This cluster of dwellings, once outlying upon Greenwich Village, came by both of its names honestly. Hand-weaving was a New York industry of some magnitude, relatively speaking, in the early years of the present century, and was carried on mainly by weavers emigrant from Scotland; and it was by some of these Scotch weavers that Paisley Place was settled and named, about the year 1822. The date is well determined, inasmuch as the settlement stands in direct relation with the yellow-fever epidemic of that year ; but whether the weavers came to Paisley in order to escape the fever, or came after the fever had passed away in order to get the benefit of low rents, is not so clear.

Mr. P. M. Wetmore, in a note upon Paisley, held to the former view. "At a little distance from where the larger merchants had made their temporary homes," he wrote, referring to Greenwich Village, "ran a secluded country lane which bore the somewhat pretentious name of Southampton Road. A convenient nook by the side of this quiet lane was chosen by a considerable number of the Scotch weavers as their place of refuge from the impending danger. They erected their modest dwellings in a row, set up their frames, spread their webs, and the shuttles flew merrily from willing fingers. With the love of Scotland strong in their hearts, and the old town from which they had wandered far away warm in their memories, they gave their new home the name of Paisley Place."

On the other hand, Mr. Devoe—who lived for many years in the immediate vicinity of Paisley, and whose knowledge in the premises was per-

NOS. 251, 253 WEST EIGHTEENTH STREET

sonal—wrote in his *Market Book:* "Many of the wooden buildings in the neighborhood [of the Jefferson Market] were suddenly put up in 1822 to accommodate the bankers, insurance and other companies, merchants, etc., who left them tenantless after the dreaded yellow-fever had subsided, which were at this period [1832] filled with weavers, laborers, and others, who sought low rents."

But whether the Scotch weavers came before or after the fever is immaterial to the point of present interest, which is that the little wooden houses on the line of the extinguished Southampton Road still stand where they were built more than seventy years ago—a fact that any person of antiquarian tendencies, sufficiently resolute not to be dashed by a bad smell or two, may verify personally by making an expedition up one of the several alleyways on the south side of Seventeenth Street west of the Sixth Avenue. And— without rising to such heights of dare-odor adventure as the search for the Weavers' Row up dubious alleyways—a house of the same period may be seen, No. 107, still standing on Seventeenth Street at the point where the Southampton Road left Paisley Place and bore away across country by the east and north.

Having, at first, Paisley as its nucleus, but being centred later upon the factory that was built at the northeast corner of Nineteenth Street and the Eighth Avenue, a scattered village grew up between Greenwich and Chelsea half a century ago — partly on the lines of the old roads and

partly on the lines of the City Plan. Many scraps
of this broadcast settlement still survive, and nearly every scrap has an interesting individuality.
Best of all are the two delightfully picturesque
wooden houses Nos. 251, 253 West Eighteenth
Street: standing far back in what once very likely were gardens, but which certainly are not
gardens now, and each having ascending to its
second story a roofed-in stair. At the northwest corner of Seventeenth Street and the Eighth
Avenue is a remnant of what, in its prime, was life
of a higher caste: the brick-front wooden dwelling, with a quaint little colonial porch having an
iron railing which would be quite perfect were
the graceful newel-posts wrought instead of cast
—a house that has an air about it, and that man-
ages to preserve even in the bedragglement of
its now sadly fallen fortunes something of the
bearing of its better days. It is far from being
in as good condition as is the row of large com-
fortable-looking frame dwellings a little west of
it on Seventeenth Street, and yet even the tradition of its former rating suffices to throw the
present undoubted well-to-do-ness of these latter
entirely in the shade—in much the way that a
battered and out-at-elbows gentleman still rises
superior to the commonplace sort of humanity
that is prosperous but has not in all its blood a
single drop of blue. Scattered along the Seventh
Avenue are half a dozen more of these trig and
seemly but not aristocratic frame houses; and at
the Eighteenth Street crossing, on the southwest

corner, is a large outcrop of now shabby wooden dwellings which very likely had their genesis in the factory that stood two blocks away to the west and north. In all this collection of remnants the oldest and the shabbiest are the most attractive — for on these is found that exalting touch of the picturesque or the romantic which is nature's gift in compensation for ruin and infirmity and broken age.

From Paisley Place the Southampton Road went northeastward by a way which still, save on Twentieth Street, is well defined. It crossed Eighteenth Street a few feet to the east of the Sixth Avenue, and there its line is recorded on the oblique western wall of the house No. 63 ; at Nineteenth Street it crossed where now are the small houses Nos. 52, 54; and on Twenty - first Street its trace is very clear in the little houses where now dwell French clear - starchers, and where once dwelt—I insist upon it—the genial landlord of Love Lane.

Being come to these old houses again, we are back very nearly to the point at which our walk began.

## LISPENARD'S MEADOWS

I

N a little hill far out in the northwestern suburb of the city of New York—so remote that it would have been gird-ed about by Hudson, Canal, and Vestry streets, had those thoroughfares then existed—
stood a century and a half ago the farm - house of Leonard Lispenard. The farm to which this house related was a portion of the estate that was known to successive generations as the Duke's Farm, the King's Farm, the Queen's Farm, and finally—when it became by gift the property of the English Church—as the Church Farm.* Lis-penard's holding, of which he was the lessee from Trinity, was styled specifically the Dominie's Bouerie, or the Dominie's Hook, and was a con-siderable property lying between the North River and a bit of swamp where now is West Broadway.

* The Corporation of Trinity claimed title to this property on the ground that it was a part of the King's Farm ; and also on the ground that it had been conveyed by the widow of the Dominie Bogardus to Governor Lovelace, and by him granted to the Eng-lish Church.

The southern line of the farm was close upon that of the present Reade Street; and thence it extended to the southern edge of the wide valley through which discharged lazily into the Hudson the stream from the Collect, or Fresh Water Pond.

Where that stream then was, now is Canal Street; and, what with the cutting down of the hills and the filling in of the hollows, one must look keenly to make sure that ever there was a valley here at all. Of the swamp, that once made a large part of the valley a dangerous quagmire, there does not remain a trace—save, possibly, in some of the cellars thereabouts; nor would any chance wayfarer along Canal Street be likely to identify this region with the meadows which came by luck and love into the possession of Leonard Lispenard, and which for more than a century—until they were wholly buried beneath the advancing piles of houses and ceased to be meadows at all—were known by his name.

For a long while after the settlement of this island the valley to the westward of the Fresh Water Pond remained in its primitive condition: a morass covered with a tangled growth of briers and bushes and young trees. It was dangerous alike to animals of four legs and of two. So many cattle wandered into it and were lost by being swamped that the Council caused it to be fenced off. So rank were the miasmatic vapors arising from it that tertian fevers, with their intermediate aguish chills, fell upon those humans luckless enough to dwell near its borders. In addition to all of which, this marshy barrier extending across two-thirds of the island confined the growth northward of the city to a narrow strip of land on the East River shore. Sooner or later, of course, the abatement of so serious a nuisance was inevitable; but that it was effected soonei rather than later was due to the discreet intelligence of Anthony Rutgers, who saw a chance to advance the city's interests (without in the least retarding his own) by turning this pestilent quag into honest dry land on condition that it should be made over to him as a free gift.

His various reasons why this modest proposition should be accepted are set forth in his petition to the King in Council—in which petition also is exhibited the condition of this region about the year 1730 — in the following terms: "The said swamp is constantly filled with standing water for which there is no natural vent, and being covered with bushes and small trees is, by the stagnation and rottenness of it, become exceedingly dangerous and of fatal consequence to all the inhabitants of the north part of the city bordering near the same, they being subject to very many diseases and distempers which, by all physicians and by long experience, are imputed to the unwholesome vapours arising thereby; and as the said swamp is upon a level with the waters of Hudson and the South [East] rivers, no person has ever yet attempted to clear the same, nor ever can under a grant thereof which is to expire

PARK AT THE FOOT OF CANAL STREET

with the next new Governor, for the expense of
clearing the same will be so great, and the length
of time in doing the same such that it never will
be attempted but by a grantee of the fee simple
thereof. and as the same can be of no benefit until it is cleared, so no person has hitherto accepted a grant of the said land, but the same hath
lain, and still remains, unimproved and unculti-
vated, to the great prejudice and annoyance of
the adjacent farms, particularly to a farm of your
petitioners, adjoining thereto, which your peti-
tioner, after having been at a great charge and
expense in settling, cannot prevail on any tenant
to take the same, or get any servants to continue
there for any time while the said swamp remains
in its present state."

Coupled with this sombre presentment of the
matter was the affidavit of one Dr. Moses Bu-
chanan to prove that things really were very bad
indeed.   He swore, did Dr. Moses, that " having
been at New York from the fifteenth day of
April, 1727, to July, 1730," he in that time had had
" several of the inhabitants who lived bordering
on the said swamp under his care for agues and
fevers which, to the best of his judgment and belief, were occasioned by the unwholesome damps
and vapours arising from the said swamp."

In short, so moving was this mass of testimony
that the Council, acceding to the request of the
accretive Anthony, granted to him out of hand
the fee to the swamp—being, in all, a parcel of
seventy acres—on condition that he should pay

for it "a moderate quit-rent," and that, also, he should "clear and drain it within a year." On the whole, this is one of the neatest operations in real estate that is recorded in the annals of New York.

But it was the son-in-law of the operator who got the good of the operation. About the time that the swamp was drained and cleared, and a good part of it made into useful meadow land, Mr. Leonard Lispenard came down from his hill to the home of his neighbor Rutgers in the valley, and there made a love-match (and at the same time made a handsome stroke for the bettering of his own fortunes) by marrying his neighbor's daughter. Out of these conditions it resulted that when Anthony Rutgers was gathered to his fathers and his realty suddenly shrunk to something less than twelve square feet of land (and even to this his only title was that of occupancy), the meadows passed to his daughter and her husband : and thenceforward were known as Lispenard's Meadows until, as I have said, their claim to any sort of a rural designation was buried beneath brick walls.

II

There were no brick walls in that vicinity in Lispenard's time. The upper end of Broadway, from about the Park onward, was a draggled bit of lane which came to a sudden ending (about where

WEST STREET NEAR CANAL

White Street now is) against a set of bars.   Up
this lane in the early mornings, and down it
again in the late afternoons, went daily sleek and
comfortable cows—going forth and back between
their aristocratic stables in the court quarter of
the city, over on Pearl and Nassau and Wall
streets, and the meadows where, bovine parlor
boarders, they feasted in luxury upon Mr. Lispenard's rich grass.

After all, it is not so very long ago that the
cows thus made their processional and recessional
journeyings to and from open pastures which now
are many miles away from even the smallest
scrap of natural green.  Several of the old gentlemen with whom of late I have talked about the
days when all the world was young — that is to
say, when they were young themselves—remember well those open meadows and those pampered
cows; and one even has told me that, by no more
of a charm than closing his eyes and thinking
about old times, he can hear again plainly the
melancholy donging of the cow-bells—a dull, sad,
droning sound—as the cows come slowly homeward down the Broadway in the sunset glow of
those vanished summer days.

It is only a life-time ago, therefore, that Lispenard's Meadows—or "Lepner's Meadows," as old-
fashioned folk had it—were a conspicuous feature
of what now is a far down part of the town.  And
from what I am told by my old gentlemen—it is
in a spirit of warm affection that I speak of them
thus possessively — I infer that at this period,

CAST-IRON NEWEL

which none of them seems to regard as at all remote, the world went very well indeed. Certainly, there were pleasures to be had in New York then which now are unobtainable. Every boy whose heart and legs are in the right places knows, for instance, how delightful it is to make a genuine expedition on skates; really to go somewhere and to come back again, and in the course of the journey to take agreeably exciting risks on ice that has not been proved. Nowadays a New York boy cannot obtain a pleasure of that sort save by first taking a railway journey; but one of my blithe old gentlemen recalls with joy how time and again he put on his skates at the Stone Bridge—that is to say, where now is the intersection of Broadway and Canal streets — and skated away over the flooded meadows, and around the base of Richmond Hill, and up the Minetta Creek (across the marsh that later was transformed into Washington Square), and so, close upon the line of

what in the fulness of time was to be the Fifth
Avenue, clear to the north of the Fourteenth
Street of the present day.

Richmond Hill—when my old gentleman thus
came skating around it in winters more than seventy years gone by—really was a hill: the southwestern outjut of the low range called the Zandtberg (that is to say, sand-hills), which swung away
in a long curve from near the present Clinton
Place and Broadway to about where Varick and
Van Dam streets now cross. The Minetta water
expanded into a large pond at the base of the
hill, and—to quote the elegant language of an
earlier day—"from the crest of this small eminence was an enticing pros-
pect: on the south, the
woods and dells and wind-
ing road from the lands
of Lispenard, through the
valley where was Borrow-
son's tavern; and on the
north and west the plains
of Greenwich Village made
up a rich prospect to gaze
on."

Yielding to the entice-
ments of the prospect,
Abraham Mortier, Esq.,
Commissary to His Majes-
ty's forces, purchased Richmond Hill about the year
1760, and built there for

WROUGHT-IRON NEWEL

himself a dwelling which was held in the taste of
the period to be vastly fine. According to the
description that has come down to us, Mr. Commissary Mortier's house was "a wooden building
of massive architecture, with a lofty portico supported by Ionic columns, the front walls dec-
orated with pilasters of the same order, and its
whole appearance distinguished by a Palladian
character of rich though sober ornament." In
other words it was one of those Grecian temples
built of two-inch pine planks, the like of which
still may be seen on the Long Island shore of
the Narrows—to the astonishment and confusion
of the intelligent foreigner for the first time coming up the bay.

During Mortier's reign on Richmond Hill that
agreeable country-seat gained a reputation for
liberal hospitality which it long maintained. Its
most distinguished guest of that period was Sir
Jeffrey, afterward Lord, Amherst, who made the
house his headquarters when he had ended those
successful campaigns which broke the power of
France in America; and which — it is well for
New-Yorkers to remember—saved a good half of
the State of New York from being now a part
of Canada.

Later, Mr. Vice-President John Adams occupied Richmond Hill—keeping up the establishment on a scale not quite so liberal as that of
the Commissary, perhaps, but with a fitting state
and dignity. A glimpse of the interior of this
household is given by Gulian C. Verplanck, writ-

ing in *The Talisman* for 1829, in his description
of a Vice-Presidential dinner-party: "There, in
the centre of the table," writes Mr. Verplanck,
"sat Vice-President Adams in full dress, with his
bag and *solitaire*, his hair frizzled out each side of
his face as you see it in Stuart's older pictures of
him. On his right sat Baron Steuben, our royalist

LISPENARD'S MEADOWS

republican disciplinarian general. On his left was
Mr. Jefferson, who had just returned from France,
conspicuous in his red waistcoat and breeches, the
fashion of Versailles. Opposite sat Mrs. Adams,
with her cheerful, intelligent face. She was placed
between the Count du Moustiers, the French am-
bassador, in his red-heeled shoes and ear-rings, and
the grave, polite, and formally bowing Mr. Van
Birket, the learned and able envoy of Holland.
There, too, was Chancellor Livingstone, then still
in the prime of his life, so deaf as to make conver-

sation with him difficult, yet so overflowing with wit, eloquence, and information that while listening to him the difficulty was forgotten. The rest were members of Congress, and of our Legislature, some of them no inconsiderable men."

The successor to Vice-President Adams in the tenancy of this estate, and the tenant with whom its name always is most closely associated, was Aaron Burr: to whom was executed a sixty-nine years' lease of the property on May 1, 1797; and who here, before and during his term as Vice-President, lived in the handsome fashion becoming to so accomplished a man of the world. It was from this house that he went forth, that July morning in the year 1804, to fight his duel with Hamilton over on the other side of the Hudson below the Wiehawken Heights — there to end, with the same shot that killed his adversary, his own public career. Presently, a political outcast, he left Richmond Hill to engage in that mysterious Southwestern project whereof the full meaning never yet has been laid bare: and so went galloping to his political death.

"The last considerable man to live at Richmond Hill," again to quote Mr. Verplanck, "was Counsellor Benzon; a man who had travelled in every part of the world, knew everything, and talked all languages." And Mr. Verplanck testifies that this gentleman maintained the hospitable traditions of the house by adding: "I recollect dining there in company with thirteen gentlemen, none of whom I ever saw before, but all pleasant fellows, all men of education and of some note—the counsellor a Norwegian, I the only American, the rest of every different nation in Europe, and no two of the same, and all of us talking bad French together."

Not many years after this cosmopolitan dinner-party, the cutting and slashing Commissioners by whom the existing City Plan was begotten

RICHMOND HILL

doomed Richmond Hill, and all the rest of the Zandtberg range, to be levelled—to the end that the lowlands thereabouts might be filled in. By ingenious methods, the old house was lowered gradually as the land was cut away from under it until it reached at last the present street level, and

found itself on the north side of Charlton Street,
a little east of Varick — which streets, being
opened, destroyed what remained to it of surrounding grounds. For a while it languished as a
road tavern; and then, I fancy thankfully, disappeared entirely that in its place the row of smug
little brick houses on Charlton Street might be
reared. The garden which lay around this ancient residence was on the hill-top, a hundred
feet or so above the present level of the land;
but there still remains, in the open block between
Charlton and King and Varick and Macdougal
streets, a surviving fragment of the garden which
lay westward of the house in its degenerate tavern
days.

### III

Close upon the southern borders of Lispenard's
Meadows were Vauxhall and Ranelagh gardens;
two vastly agreeable places of genteel amusement to which resorted the gay gentlefolk of
New York's frolic past. These gardens were in
humble imitation of their famous prototypes in
London, and provided entertainment of a like
sort: music, a hall for dancing, lamplit groves in
which to wander between the dances, and " tables
spread with various delicacies "—all for the benefit of a " company gayly drest, looking satisfied,"
as Goldsmith phrased it when describing the
older gardens in his *Citizen of the World.*

The New York Vauxhall was known originally

NO. 210 WEST TENTH STREET

as the Bowling Green Gardens, and as such—being shown on Lyne's map—certainly was in existence as far back as the year 1729. It received its more pretentious name about the middle of the last century, and continued to be a place of fashionable resort during the ensuing forty years. With the revival of the city's prosperity, when the Revolutionary war was well ended, the land occupied by the gardens became too valuable to be used for such merely decorative purposes. Gradually the pleasure-grounds were diminished in size by encroaching buildings, and at last only the old Vauxhall house remained. This, being still a tavern, stood at the corner of Greenwich and Warren streets for many years — gradually settling down through the various grades of respectability until it reached a level at which it most judiciously disappeared.

Ranelagh — in which pleasure-resort, presumably, Leonard Lispenard and his wife had a moneyed interest—had a handsome beginning and a better end. It was the transformed homestead of Colonel Rutgers, Lispenard's father-in-law, and it remained respectable throughout the whole of its career.

About the year 1730—at the very time that he began to lay his plans for acquiring the meadows without having to pay for them—Colonel Rutgers built him a prodigiously fine dwelling near the present corner of Thomas Street and Broadway; and there he lived in a becomingly stately fashion during the twenty years that he remained a citizen of this city and this world. "He surrounded his habitation," writes the engaging Mr. Valentine, "with elegant shrubbery in the geometrical style of rural gardening of those days. Long walks, bordered with boxwood and shaded and perfumed with flowering shrubs, extended in various directions in the parterre bordering the house; the favorite orchard extended along the southerly side of the mansion, while the pasture-lands and cultivated fields extended towards the north." It was "a charming rural residence," Mr. Valentine declares; and adds that " even in after-years, when its quiet and domestic characteristics had given place to the festive incidents attached to a public resort, the advertisement of the proprietor expressed it as judged to be the most rural and pleasing retreat in the city."

Colonel Rutgers died about the year 1750, and very soon after his death "the domestic characteristics" vanished from his home, and "the festive incidents attached to a public resort" took their place. This transformation was effected under the proprietorship of one John Jones, who seems to have been a person of sanguine temperament and also not over-modest: if one may judge by the advertisements in *The Weekly Post Boy*, in which he handsomely credits himself with having spent his money in the most lavish fashion to the end that in every way his patrons should be well served. However, in that his Ranelagh possessed "all conveniences for breakfasting, and every entertainment for ladies and gentlemen"; that it had " a complete band in attendance every Monday and Thursday during the summer in a large dancing-hall," and that at all times it offered to its patrons " ornamental gardens laid out in the geometrical style," Mr. John Jones seems to have been more or less justified in saying, as he un-

PUMP ON GREENWICH STREET, BELOW CANAL

hesitatingly did say, that it was " a popular resort of very elegant excellence."

The rise of Ranelagh, I fancy, had much to do with the decline of Vauxhall. The new gardens not only were more accessible than the old ones, but they started with a certain elegant prestige :

due to the fact that the polite society of the metropolis was invited by the enterprising Jones to
continue to visit for a money consideration at a
house where it long had been accustomed to visit
on the score of pure friendliness—which invita-
tion the more readily was accepted because of the
delicate relish that there was in exchanging genial " wonders " (between the dances, while sipping
daintily at arrack punch) as to how " dear Mrs.
Lispenard ever *could* have brought herself to
permit her father's home to be used in such a
way !" Certainly, while they lasted, the gardens
were an unqualified success, attracting always
the better class of society and taking the leading place (to quote Jones again) " among those
suburban places of amusement where music,
dancing, and feasting contribute their share in
the amusements of the hour." And, finally, they
had the good-fortune to die a genteel death in
the station of life to which they had been born ;
that is to say, this Ranelagh on Broadway (there
was another Ranelagh, later, out on the Bowery)
ceased to exist while still a fashionable resort,
and did not, as did its less fortunate rival, go
reeling down hill to a ruinous ending in the slums.

About the year 1765 Brannan's Gardens were
established over on the north side of the Meadows, near the present crossing of Hudson and
Spring streets. But this establishment, in the
main, was a daytime resort and made its account
out of thirsty wayfarers — whereof there were
many in that part of the island and in those cord-

ial days. Close in front of it ran the Greenwich
Road, the river-side drive along which went a gallant parade of fashionable New York in the bright
summer and autumn weather and which in winter was all a-jingle with the bells of sleighs. The
world went in a simpler and heartier way then,
and the road-side taverns had a place in the social economy that was very far from low. I have
quoted in another paper the appreciative com-
ments of the Rev. Mr. Burnaby (an English traveller who surveyed this city about one hundred
and forty years ago) upon the Kissing Bridge
—an institution which evidently struck him favorably—and his careful explanation of the conditions which made kissing-bridges possible also
explains how such outlying resorts as Brannan's
Gardens were supported. " The amusements,"
writes his Reverence, " are balls and sleighing-
parties in the winter, and in the summer going in
parties upon the water and fishing, or making
excursions into the country. There are several
houses pleasantly situated up the East River,
near New York, where it is common to have turtle feasts. These happen once or twice a week.
Thirty or forty gentlemen and ladies meet and
dine together; drink tea in the afternoon; fish
and amuse themselves till evening, and then return home in Italian chaises (the fashionable carriage in this and most parts of America, Virginia
excepted, where they chiefly make use of coaches,
and those commonly drawn by six horses), a gentleman and lady in each chaise."

Such a party as this, coming back about sunset from Turtle Bay, would be pretty certain to prolong the drive by switching off from the Post Road (now Broadway) at Love Lane (now Twenty-first Street) and so across to the Fitzroy Road (close on the line of the present Eighth Avenue) and down to Greenwich Village, and thence down the Greenwich Road towards home. And such a party, also, even though it had stopped for a sup at the tavern which I am confident stood at the corner of Love Lane and the Southampton Road, and for another sup at "The Old Grapevine" in Greenwich, would find in these suppings only another reason for stopping at Brannan's for just one sup more.

THE LOCKSMITH'S SIGN

And how brave a sight it must have been when —the halt for refreshments being ended — the long line of carriages got under way again and went dashing along the causeway over Lispenard's green meadows, while the silvered harness of the horses and the brilliant varnish of the Italian chaises gleamed and sparkled in the rays of

nearly level sunshine from the sun that was setting there a hundred years and more ago!

IV

For so long a while did the cow-bars across
Broadway, a little north of Warren Street, check
absolutely the advance of the city on the western
side of the island that within the present century
the ghosts of those turtle feasters, in the ghosts
of their Italian chaises, might have driven across
Lispenard's meadows without perceiving any
change at all.   Actually, the
levelling undertaken at the
instance of the Commissioners was completed less than
sixty years ago; and a still
shorter time has passed since
solid blocks of houses were
erected on the land which
these radical reformers de-
spoiled of its natural beauty,
and then proudly described
as "reclaimed."

AN OLD-TIME KNOCKER

The secretary and engi-
neer to the devastating Commissioners, old Mr. John
Randel — who kept up a
show of youthfulness to the last by signing his
name always John Randel, Jun.—has left on record a characteristically precise description of the

region between the Canal and Greenwich Village
as it was just before the levelling process began ;
that is to say, as it was a trifle over eighty years
ago.

"In going from the city to our office [in Green-
wich] in 1808 and 1809," he writes, under date of
April 6, 1864, "I generally crossed a ditch cut
through Lispenard's salt meadow (now a culvert
under Canal Street) on a plank laid across it for
a crossing place about midway between a stone
bridge on Broadway with a narrow embankment
at each end connecting it with the upland, and
an excavation then being made at, and said to
be for, the foundation of the present St. John's
Church on Varick Street. From this crossing-
place I followed a well-beaten path leading from
the city to the then village of Greenwich, passing
over open and partly fenced lots and fields, not
at that time under cultivation, and remote from
any dwelling-house now remembered by me except
Colonel Aaron Burr's former country-seat, on elevated ground, called Richmond Hill, which was
about one hundred or one hundred and fifty
yards west of this path, and was then occupied
as a place of refreshment for gentlemen taking a
drive from the city. Its site is now in Charlton
Street, between Varick and Macdougal streets. I
continued along this main path to a branch path
diverging from it to the east, south of Manetta
water (now Minetta Street), which branch path I
followed to Herring Street [now Bleecker Street],
passing on my way there, from about two hundred

to two hundred and fifty yards west, the country residence of Colonel Richard Varick, on elevated ground east of Manetta water, called 'Tusculum,' the site of which is now on Varick Place,
on Sullivan Street, between Bleecker and Houston
streets.   On Broadway, north of Lispenard's salt
meadow, now Canal Street, to Sailors' Snug Harbor, a handsome brick building called by that
name, erected on elevated ground near the bend
in Broadway near the present Tenth Street, and
formerly the residence of Captain Randall ; . . .
and from the Bowery road westward to Manetta
water, there were only a few scattered buildings,
except country residences which were built back
from Broadway with court - yards and lawns of
trees and shrubs in front of them." All of
which is quite in keeping with the statement
of one of my old gentlemen that he remembers
looking south from the stoop of his father's house
on Leroy Street, in Greenwich, across a broad
expanse of open country to the distant city ; and
east, also across open country, to the gallows
which stood within the present limits of Washington Square.

V

It is a fact illustrative of the high-pressure way
in which this city of New York is run that the
Canal Street region, whereof the youthfulness is
proved by the foregoing testimony, already is old.

In a fashion that would make a European city dizzy, it has dashed through all the phases which mark the progress from youth to age; and already, in no more than a man's lifetime, has passed on into decay.

Eighty years ago it was suburban and obscure. Twenty years later, Hudson Square having been laid out and St. John's Church built, it began to be fashionable. In another twenty years—the square being then surrounded by the wide-fronted houses of which many stately wrecks remain—it was one of the most gravely respectable parts of the town: and for more than a decade it remained at this aristocratical high-water mark. Then began its slow decline—which ended in a sudden and irrevocable plunge in the year 1869, when the Hudson River Railroad Company crushed the region utterly, so far as its fitness to be an abiding-place of polite society was concerned, by clapping down four acres of freight-station over the whole of the luckless park. Only one man of position stayed by the wreck, and even may be said to have gone down with it. This was John Ericsson, the builder of the *Monitor*, who continued in his home of many years on St. John's Park until, holding up to the last in that frowsy and bustling region its traditional calm respectability, he died there only a little while ago.

To-day, the dwellers upon St. John's Park are mainly foreigners: a few Germans, but more Italians—as even a blind man, possessing a travelled

CANAL STREET AND ST. JOHN'S CHURCH

and intelligent nose, would know by the aggressive presence of several distinctively Neapolitan
smells.  The stately houses, swarming with this
unwashed humanity, are sunk in such squalor
that upon them rests ever an air of melancholy
devoid of hope.  They are tragedies in mellow-
toned brick and carved wood-work that once was
very beautiful.  To them relief can come only in
the form of destruction, and the only destruction
that can restore their self-respect—though only
in the moment of their final agony—by making
them for an instant clean again, is fire.  Until
this happy fate comes to them, their portion is
despair.

Serene in the midst of this grime of humanity
and trade, the gravely beautiful church—standing at ease in its quiet, grassy yard—maintains a
calm nobleness: while from its steeple its bells
ring out as clearly and as sweetly as in the days
when—as one of my old gentlemen tells me—
their melody went floating across the meadows
clear away to Greenwich whenever there blew a
southerly wind.  When the clock bell strikes
noon, nowadays, there is a great commotion before the church in Varick Street, as the Italian
stevedores employed in the railway station wheel
away their trucks, and the drays and carts scatter,
and there comes an outburst—jetting a strain of
shrillness into the general noise—of yelping little
boys from St. John's parish school.

The Presbyterian church that once stood near
by in Laight Street long since closed its doors.

Being but a little church, and so close to a big one, it was styled by the irreverent "St. John's Kitchen": yet was there very eloquent preaching within its walls when Dr. Samuel Cox occupied its pulpit, and, with sometimes eccentric but always very earnest vehemence, urged his hearers to be folded and saved with the sheep rather than cast adrift with the goats to be damned !

By an odd twist of destiny, it is mainly to the aristocratic houses on the Square that an evil fate has come. The less pretentious structures thereabouts have sunk only to the level of lodging-houses; and many of them even—as is manifested by their superior air of self-respecting neatness — still are private dwellings. North of Canal Street, over what once was Lispenard's land and on northward into Greenwich Village, there is a succession of quiet little streets filled with quiet little houses, in each of which, for the most part, a single family dwells. About this region there never has been the slightest pretence to style. Land values here always have been low, and much of the property can be acquired only on leasehold from Trinity. From the beginning, therefore, it has been a region of modest homes; and if there is an American quarter anywhere in New York it is here.

The little brick houses of two, and two and a half, and three stories, date from about forty years ago; but among them, here and there, wooden dwellings survive from a much earlier time. At the corner of Varick and Spring streets;

on Dominick Street off from Clark; on Desbrosses
Street off from Hudson; at Nos. 6 and 8 Macdougal; at the head of King—and at many other
points which will well repay looking for — are
wooden survivals which cannot fail to cheer the
heart of every lover of ancient things. The view
at the head of King Street, by-the-way—over the
low wooden houses to the towering west front of
the church of Sant' Antonio di Padua—at about
eleven o'clock in the morning, when is had the
right effect of light and shade, is one of the most
satisfying views in New York.

But this American quarter, as is implied by
this mention of a church dedicated to an Italian
saint, is sandwiched in between the abiding-places
of highly foreign foreigners. West Street, from
Canal north to Christopher, being the docking-
place of the principal lines of trans - Atlantic
steamers, is naturally cosmopolitan: with the German tongue and the German beer-saloon a little
in the lead. On this international thoroughfare is
to be heard at all times such a chattering of out-
landish tongues as to suggest the immediate
proximity of the Tower of Babel; and the same is
true of the little park at the point where West
Street is joined by Canal. From the park, a mere
step across the street sets one aboard a Pacific
Mail steamer: and so in possession of fascinating
possibilities of travel along all the western coasts
of both Americas, and out yet farther westward
to the Pacific islands, and so to China and Japan.
Merely to sit for a while in that park is to give

one the feeling of having gone upon several long journeys ; and this feeling is greatly intensified if one is lucky enough (and 'tis easy done) to fall into talk with one of the old men who come here to sun themselves on crisp autumn days. These old men always are more than willing to talk to any reasonably sympathetic person about the fortunes and the misfortunes of their ancient lives ; and they not unlikely—being moved thereto by the thrilling influence of the near-by shipping, which upon souls of a certain romantic constitution works always an exalting charm — may tell strange stories of desperate adventure in far-off countries or in the waste and hidden places of the sea.

But toward this park my disposition is cordial on other grounds. It is the one bit of green hereabouts to keep alive the memory of the meadows which only a hundred years ago stretched east to Broadway, and south (on the river side of Church Street) almost to the Hospital, and north up the Minetta valley beyond Washington Square. And sometimes, sitting there when no imaginative old man is at hand for my entertainment, I like to close my eyes and fall to thinking how pleasant a walk I might take—into a sort of contemporaneous antiquity — could I but stroll arm-in-arm with the strong Dutch spirit of Colonel Anthony Rutgers, or with the lighter French shade of Mr. Leonard Lispenard, over the region where their meadows used to be.

## THE BATTERY

WHEN Hendrick Hudson came sailing into the mouth of the river that thenceforward was to be known by his name, on that September day in the year 1609, almost the whole of what now is called "the Battery" was under water at high tide. And it is a fact—notwithstanding the thundering of guns which has gone on thereabouts, and the blustering name that the locality has worn for more than two centuries—that not a single one of New York's enemies ever would have been a whit the worse had the tides continued until this very moment to cover the Battery twice a day! Actually, the entire record of this theoretically offensive institution — whereof the essential and menacing purpose, of course, was that somebody or something should be battered by it—has been an aggregation of gentle civilities which would have done credit to a rather exceptionally mild-mannered lamb.

Most appropriately, this affable offspring of Bellona came into existence as the friendly prop to a still more weak-kneed fort. For reasons best known to themselves, the Dutch clapped down what they intended should be the main defence of this island upon a spot where a fort—save as a place of refuge against the assaults of savages—

was no more than a bit of military bric-à-brac. Against the savages it did, on at least one occasion, serve its purpose ; yet had even these attacked it resolutely they must surely have carried it : since each of the Dutch governors has left upon record bitter complainings of the way in which it was invaded constantly by cows and goats who triumphantly marched up its earthen ramparts in nibbling enjoyment of its growth of grass. When the stress of real war came—with the landing of the English forces in the year 1664 —the taking of this absurd fort was a mere bit of bellicose etiquette : a polite changing of garrisons, of fealty, and of flags.

Later, when Governor Stuyvesant very properly was hauled over the coals for the light-handed way in which he had relinquished a valuable possession, his explanation did not put the matter in much better shape. " The Fort," he wrote, " is situated in an untenable place, where it was located on the first discovery of New Netherland, for the purpose of resisting an attack of the barbarians rather than an assault of European arms ; having, within pistol-shot on the north and southeast sides, higher ground than that on which it stands, so that, notwithstanding the walls and works are raised highest on that side, people standing and walking on that high ground can see the soles of the feet of those on the esplanades and bastions of the Fort."

Having themselves so easily captured it, the English perceived the need of doing something

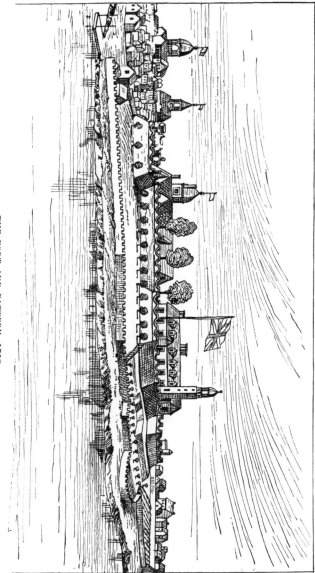

THE FORT AND BATTERY, 1750

to the Fort that would enable them to hold it against the Dutch in the probable event of these last trying to win it back again. The radical course of abandoning it to the cows and goats and building a new fort upon higher ground—on, for instance, the high bluff above the river-side where Trinity Church now stands — would have been the wisest action that could have been taken in the premises; but the very human tendency to try to improve an existing bad thing, rather than to create a new good thing, restrained them from following out this one possible line of effectual reform. Raising the walls of the Fort was talked about for a while; until Colonel Cartwright, the engineer, put a stopper upon this suggestion by declaring, in effect, that taking the walls up to the height of those of Jericho would not make the place tenable. And then, after more talk, the decision was reached that to build a battery under the walls of the Fort would be to create defences "of greater advantage and more considerable than the Fort itself": whereupon this work was taken in hand by General Leverett and carried briskly to completion—and from that time onward the Battery has been part and parcel of New York.

The amount of land which then constituted the Battery was trifling: as is shown by the statement in Governor Dongan's report to the Board of Trade (1687), "the ground that the Fort stands upon and that belongs to it contains in quantity about two acres or thereabouts." The high-water mark of that period would be indicated roughly by a line drawn with a slight curve to the westward from the foot of the present Greenwich Street to the intersection of the present Whitehall and Water streets. All outside of this line is made land which has been won from the river, the greater part of it within the past forty years, by filling in over the rocks which fringed this southwestern shore.

This primitive Battery was but a small affair, loosely constructed and lightly armed. As to its armament, the report of the survey ordered in the year 1688 contains the item: "Out the Fort, under the flag-mount, near the water-side, 5 demi-culverins;" and its inherent structural weakness is shown by the fact that only five years after its erection—that is to say, in 1689, when Leisler's righteous revolt made the need for strong defences urgent—its condition was so ruinous as to be beyond repair; wherefore it was replaced by "a half-moon mounting seven great guns."

As the event proved, this half-moonful of guns would have satisfied for almost another century all that might have been (but was not) required of artillery in this neighborhood. But the times were troublous across seas; and the Leisler matter had proved that questions of European abstract faith and concrete loyalty might exercise a very tumultuous and dismal influence upon American lives. And so the prudent New-Yorkers, about the year 1693, decided to bring their waterside defences to a condition of high efficiency by

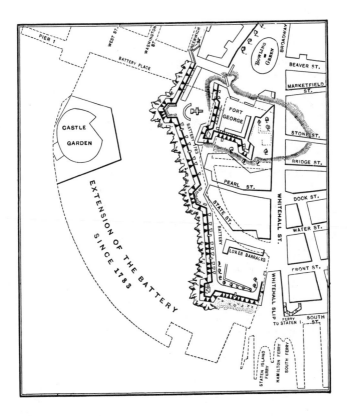

building " a great battery of fifty guns on the out-
most point of rocks under the Fort, so situated as
to command both rivers," and, incidentally, to defy
the world.

In the mere planning of this nobly defiant undertaking there seems to have been gained so
comforting a sense of security that its realization
was not arrived at for nearly half a century—as
appears from Governor Clarke's statement (1738):
" There is a battery which commands the mouth
of the harbor, whereon may be mounted 50 cannon. This is new, having been built but three
years, but it wants finishing." In the course of
the ensuing thirty years—possibly even sooner—
the finishing touches seem to have been supplied;
at least, the Battery is shown as completed on
Ratzen's map of 1767; and it is certain that these
defences were in effective condition while New
York was held by the English during the Revolutionary War. Indeed, during the Revolutionary period the Battery really was a battery of
some importance: as may be seen by the accom-
panying plan, showing a line of works extending
from the foot of Greenwich Street along all the
water-front to Whitehall Slip. But what made
the Battery harmless at that, potentially, most
belligerent period of its history was precisely
what has made it harmless throughout the whole
of its kindly career: the absolute absence of an
enemy at whom to discharge its guns.

When the Revolutionary War was ended the
nonsensical Fort at last was demolished—which

was good riddance to amusingly bad rubbish—
and with it the Battery went too. Why this last
was razed is not at all clear. Unlike the Fort, it
was not in anybody's way, and it was not a military laughing-stock. On the contrary, it occupied an otherwise unused corner of the island,
and so well commanded the entrance to the East
and North rivers that it was saved from being
deadly dangerous only by the persistent absence
of a foe. Indeed—in theory, at least—it was so
reasonable a bit of fortification that when we
went to fighting England again, in the year 1812,
it immediately was built up anew. During that
period of warfare, of course, nothing more mur-
derous than blank cartridge was fired from its
eager guns; but there it was — waiting with its
usual energy for the chance to hurt somebody
which (also as usual) never came.

Meanwhile there had been set up in this region another military engine of destruction which,
adapting itself to the gentler traditions of its en-
vironment, never came to blows with anybody,
but led always a life of peaceful usefulness that is
not yet at an end. This was the Southwest Battery: that later was to be known honorably as
Castle Clinton; that still later was to become
notable, and then notorious, as Castle Garden;
and that at the present time is about to take a
fresh start in respectability as the Aquarium.

It is not easy to realize, nowadays—as we see
this chunky little fort standing on dry ground,
with a long sweep of tree-grown park in its rear

—that when it was built, between the years 1807 and 1811, it was a good hundred yards out from the shore. Its site, ceded by the city to the Federal Government, was a part of the outlying reef known as "the Capske"; and when the fort was finished the approach to it was by way of a long bridge in which there was a draw. The armament of this stronghold was twenty-eight 32-pounders: and when these went banging off their blank-cartridges in salutes, and clouds of powder-smoke went rolling down to leeward, there was not a more pugnacious-looking little fume of a fort to be found in all Christendom.

The Battery Park, or Battery Walk, as it indifferently was called, of that period was a crescent-shaped piece of ground of about ten acres—being less than half the size of the Battery Park of the present day—which ended at the water-side in a little bluff, capped by a wooden fence, with a shingly beach beyond. Along the edge of the bluff the earthworks of the year 1812 were erected, and were neither more nor less useful than the wooden fence which they replaced. However, what with the grim array of guns lowering over the earthen parapet, and the defiant look of the obese little fort, the New York of that epoch must have worn to persons approaching it from the seaward—being for the most part oystermen and the crews of Jersey market-boats—a most alarmingly swaggering and dare-devil sort of an air.

Yet was there a cheerful silver lining to these

THE BATTERY, 1822

dismally black clouds of war. In his admirable monograph upon " New York City during the War of 1812–15," Mr. Guernsey writes: " In the summer of 1812 there was occasionally music after supper, at about 6.30 P.M., at the Battery flag-staff," which "stood at the southeast end of the Battery parade, and was surrounded by an octagon enclosure of boards, with seats inside and a roof to shelter from the weather. Refreshments and drinks were served from this building, and a large flag was displayed from the pole at appropriate times." Never, surely, was there a more charming exhibition of combined gentleness and strength than then was made : when the brave men of New York, night after night, gallantly invited the beautiful women their fellow-citizens to partake of "refreshments and drinks" close beside the stern rows of deadly cannon, and beneath the flag to defend which, as the women themselves, they were sworn ! In all history there is no parallel to it : unless, perhaps, it might be likened to the ball and the battle of Waterloo—with the battle left out.

Even the New-Yorkers of that period—whose infusion of Dutch blood still was too strong to permit them easily to assimilate ideas—could not but perceive that as a place of recreation, where refreshments and drinks could be had to a musical accompaniment, the real use of their psuedo-Battery at last had been found. Out of this rational view of the situation came the project—formulated soon after Castle Clinton was re-ceded

to the city, in the year 1822, upon the translation
of the Federal military headquarters to Governor's
Island — to make over the fort into a place of
amusement; which project was realized, and Castle Garden came into existence, in the year 1824.
From that time onward, through all the phases of
its variegated career—as concert-hall, place of civic
assembly, theatre, immigrant dépôt, armory—the
building at least has been able to account for itself on grounds whereof the mere statement would
not, as in the days when it was pretending to be
a fort, instantly excite a grin.

With the departure from Castle Clinton of the
last of its 32-pounders went also the last vestige
of an excuse on the part of the Battery for retaining its Sir Lucius O'Trigger of a name.   But in
that region, fortunately, old names live on.   There
are the Beaver's Path and the Maiden's Lane, the
first of which has ceased to be the exclusive property of beavers, and the second of maidens, for more
than two and a half centuries; there is the Wall
Street, whence the wall departed about A.D. 1700;
and there is the Bowling Green, where bowls have
not been played for well on toward two hundred
years.   With these admirable precedents to stay
and to strengthen it in use, there is no fear that
the name of the Battery soon will pass away.   And
even should the brave name be lost in the course
of ages, still, surely, must be preserved always the
gracious legend of those peaceful guns which never thundered at a foe.

## THE DEBTORS' PRISON

BUT a trifle more than sixty years ago one of
the most agreeably edifying sights of this
town—to which country relatives come up for a
holiday might be taken with a pleasurable advantage — was the Debtors' Prison. This structure
stood (and in a revamped state still stands, being
the present Hall of Records) at the northeast corner of what now is the City Hall Park; but before
it came to be employed in what, for a prison, was
so genteel a fashion it had led but a shabby, and
in one period of its existence an even execrable,
career.

In the early decades of the past century the
criminals of New York were lodged (with a
shrewd thrust of prophetic sarcasm) in the City
Hall: which building then stood on the site now
occupied by the United States Treasury on Wall
Street. As early as the year 1724 the impossi-
bility (even more conspicuously obvious at a
later date) of confining the City Hall criminals
within that edifice became apparent, and in 1727
four men were appointed " to watch it to prevent
escapes." But in 1740 complaints were made
that even the walls and the watchers together
did not suffice to restrain the prisoners; and at
last, in the year 1756, an Act of Assembly was

procured enabling the corporation to provide
means for the erection of a jail with walls of such
solidity that through them prisoners could not
ooze away.

The site chosen for this structure was in " The
Fields"—whereof the surviving remnant is the
present City Hall Park—and the original plan
called for a building two stories in height and
about fifty feet square. While in process of construction the addition of a third story with a "cu-
pola" (which later became a famous outlook for
fires) was decided upon; and in this shape the
New Jail, as it then and thereafter was called,
came into existence and certainly was in use
by the year 1764: at which time the whip-
ping-post, stocks, cage, and pillory were brought
from Wall Street and were set up in front of it,
while the gallows—less constantly in requisition
—stood a little retired in its rear. Close beside
it (on the site where now stands the City Hall)
stood the Poor-house, that had been erected in
the year 1735; and about the year 1775 the
Bridewell was built, in a line with these cheerful
structures, over beside Broadway. Thus adorned,
" The Fields"—being so obviously the terminal
station of various sorts of criminal careers—was a
veritable object-lesson in morality.

The evil fame of the New Jail was acquired
in the time of the Revolutionary War. During
the English occupation of this island it was used
as a military prison under the charge of the rep-
robate Provost-Marshal Cunningham: and so came

to be known as the Provost, or the Provost Jail.
Of the truly horrible cruelties to which were sub-
jected the Americans there confined—who for the
most part were either officers or civilians of gentle blood—it is needless now to speak. Sleeping
dogs of so ugly a sort very well may lie. And,
moreover, whatever was the sum of this particular score against Great Britain we wrote it off
the books forever on the 28th of April of the
year 1893: when the sailors of Queen Victoria
—marching where no armed Englishman has
marched since November 25, 1783—were cheered
to the echo from the doors and windows of the
very building in which American patriots were
dealt with most foully by the servants of that
gracious woman's graceless grandfather, King
George the Third.

When the war was ended the Provost reverted
to more legitimate uses again; but under regula-
tions which sent all the common criminals to the
Bridewell, and made the New Jail merely a place
of genteel detention for prisoners for debt: those
thriftless (or, possibly, over-thrifty) persons who
were for dancing through the world at the charges
of anybody whom they could induce to pay their
piper; and whose simple concept of economical
finance was never to pay a piper, nor anybody else,
for themselves. That this class was represented
over-liberally in the New York of a hundred years
ago might be inferred from the fact that between
January 2d and December 3d of the year 1788 no
less than 1162 debtors were sent to prison; in

other words—the population then being about 25,000—one citizen in every twenty, or thereabouts, went to jail for debt. Fortunately for the reputation of the New-Yorkers of the last century, however, these figures—which I find in a petition addressed by the Association for the Relief of Distressed Debtors to the General Assembly—are misleading when taken without their qualifying context. The purport of the petition was to exhibit the injury done to the community by "the confinement of debtors for small sums," and its major premise was the fact that of the 1162 commitments specified no less than 716 were "for sums recoverable before a justice of the peace, and many of these under twenty shillings." Very reasonably, therefore, the memorialists urge that the confinement of debtors for such slight cause inures greatly to the injury of the community : " as thereby the certain profit which would arise to society from the labour of the debtor is sacrificed, for an indefinite time, to the precarious prospect of recovering a debt which the creditor, in most instances, has improvidently suffered to be contracted, and which very often does not amount to one-fourth of the value the public would derive from the labour of the debtor during the time of his confinement"—all of which, save the delightful and also astute saddling of the responsibility for the debt upon the "improvident" creditor, is very much what Solon had to say upon the same subject rather more than two thousand years earlier in the history of the world.

As rearranged after the Revolution, the Debtors' Prison consisted of twelve wards, six on the first and six on the second floor; and with these last a chapel in which the debtors were privileged to hear prayers read every Thursday. Obviously, the large number of committed debtors could not be accommodated in this building; and to meet the requirements of the case the plan was adopted—from the English system—of ideally increasing the size of the prison by permitting well-to-do debtors (who had snatched from their burning fortunes a comforting brand or two wherewith to pay for such privileges) to live outside of it, but within what were termed its "limits." In Blunt's *Strangers' Guide to the City of New York* for the year 1817, the limits of the Debtors' Prison are described as extending to "about 160 acres," and as subject to alteration by the judges of the Court of Common Pleas; to which is added the statement that "permission to reside in the limits may be obtained for fifty cents and finding proper security to the satisfaction of the Gailor; but this is only granted after judgment has been obtained."

At that period, according to the guide-book, there were "only thirty-five prisoners within the walls; and outside, within the limits, between five and six hundred." These figures relate specifically to August, 1817, and presumably show a considerably smaller number of prisoners than were on the rolls a few months earlier—inasmuch as the Act of Assembly of April 15, 1817, provid-

ed that " any person confined in this prison for a
debt not exceeding $25, exclusive of costs, upon
applying to any judge or justice of the city, and
making oath that his real or personal estate does
not exceed in value $25 over and above the arti-
cles exempted by law from seizure in execution,
is entitled to be set at liberty."

This humane law — which virtually complied
with the petition of 1788—so materially modified
the conditions in regard to debtors that the need
for a debtors' prison as a separate institution practically disappeared.  For another dozen years the
New Jail remained in existence ; but with a constantly increasing exhibition of the extravagance
involved in maintaining so considerable an establishment for so small an end.  Indeed, a genial
tradition declares that the prison was continued
in commission through these later years not in
the interest of the prisoners, but in the interest
of their jailer, the kindly and prodigiously stout
Pappy Lownds—who was not fitted to discharge
the duties of any other office in the gift of the
corporation ; and who, even had there been another berth available for him, was too fat to be
moved.

In the year 1830 (hearts by that time having
grown harder, perhaps) this arcadian state of affairs was brought to an end by the urgent request
of the then Register for a fire-proof building in
which to house the city records, and by the phe-
nomenally prompt decision of the City Council
to gratify his request : out of which conditions

ENTRANCE TO BROOKLYN BRIDGE AND HALL OF RECORDS

came the result that the New Jail not only disappeared, but that—being cut down a story and
encased in new outer walls—it was replaced by
an edifice which long was regarded by compla-
cent New-Yorkers as a prodigy of classic archi-
tectural art.

After the initial burst of hurry the work went
on so temperately that the requirements of the
original plan have not been executed completely
even now, at the end of sixty-four years. However, by the summer of 1832 the building was so
far advanced that it could be used as a temporary
cholera hospital; and a year later the Register,
the Comptroller, the Surrogate, and the Street
Commissioners were housed together within its
walls. All of these offices long since were crowded out by the records—the Surrogate in 1858, the
Street Commissioners in 1859, and in 1869 the
Comptroller. That the remaining tenant has
made exceedingly bad use of his exclusive property is patent to the eyes and nose of whoever
ventures within its dirty precincts; nor will such
adventurer question the tradition of the office
that within it are recorded all the bad smells
which have been known on this island from the
earliest Dutch times.

Fortunately this defilement of the interior of
the Hall of Records has not affected its exterior,
which essentially is unchanged since Recorder
Riker took possession of his new quarters sixty
years ago. Yet probably not many people, looking at this modest little building nowadays, even

faintly imagine—what actually was the fact—that when it was newly finished it was the most beautiful structure upon the island, and was the pride and open boast of the city of New York. A few keen observers there must be—among the million or so of human beings passing it every day—who perceive the symmetry of its proportions, its admirable mass, its simple elegance, and who wonder whence these classic excellences were derived; and such discriminating observers will not be surprised when they know its genesis. Actually, the little Hall of Records is patterned upon the mighty temple of Diana of Ephesus—that majestic Artemision which would cover (should Cherisiphon come alive again and set up his masterpiece here in New York) not an odd corner of the City Hall Park, but the whole of Union Square—and so does it come honestly by its heritage of grace.

## OLD-TIME PLEASURE-GARDENS

EVEN in the serene period of the Dutch domination of this island, its inhabitants were wont to betake themselves—in a gentle and semi-somnolent fashion—to rural joys. At the very first, while savages still roved the region north of where Trinity now stands, and were liable to take scalps, if occasion offered, in the wild woodland where now is the City Hall Park, the Dutchmen of Manhattoes discreetly smoked their pipes and drank their schnapps close under the shelter of the guns of the Fort: that brave structure which defied mankind in general, and never was carried by assault save by escalading squadrons of pigs and cows in quest of grass. And 'twas a lesson in peaceful happiness to behold the founders of this city sitting with a broad firmness—as became their great natures and the nether configuration of their substantial bodies—on the benches in the garden behind Martin Krieger's tavern on the Bowling Green, or in front of Aunt Metje Wessel's tavern on the Perel Straat, calmly enjoying the beauties of nature in the early evening freshness of those summer days whereon the sun went down slowly, as though loath to lose sight of them, more than two centuries and a half ago.

A little later, when Dutch valor had thrust the

savages back into the remote wilderness beyond
Harlem, that longing for rural pleasures which
ever since has characterized the innocent inhabitants of this town fully declared itself; and to
satisfy it Wolfert Webber built his tavern, in the
midst of a fair garden, near the then famous Tea-
water Spring and close to where now is Chatham
Square.    Tea-water, as such, was not in any great
request at this suburban resort ; but of warm
afternoons the potential tea-water was abundantly useful — coming cool from the spring in great
jugs of Delft utterance — for the compounding
of beverages of a sturdier sort better fitted for
the refreshment of a race engaged in conquer-
ing standing - room in a savage land.    And with
these liquid pleasures were to be had also—at
the hands of the skilled Vrouw Webber — all
manner of toothsome cakes and pies.    Moreover,
in a grave and seemly fashion — such exercise
used judiciously being an agreeable stimulant to
both thirst and hunger—the placid revellers who
here assembled were wont to play at bowls.

In truth, it was a bit got adrift out of Arcady,
this tree-bowered tavern of Wolfert Webber's :
whence, in addition to all the happiness there
was immediately about it, there was wafted far
away toward Harlem, when the soft south winds
of summer were a-blowing, such an aromatic and
delicious odor of Holland spirits as was fit to
bring tears of longing into the eyes of every wayfarer home-coming down the Bowery Road.    And
when the Kissing Bridge was built, across the rill

running from the Tea-water Spring, what with the promise held out by Wolfert's jolly, thick-set, Dutch black bottles and by the toll that lawfully could be taken at the bridge from the jolly, thick-set, Dutch fair maidens on the way homeward in the dusk, there was not on the whole continent of North America a pleasure-place more justly or more generously esteemed.

But the Kissing Bridge, which came into existence about the time that the seventeenth century was laid to rest and became a back number in the files of Time, was an institution begotten of the new English race which forcibly assumed possession of this island and made New Amsterdam over into New York in the year 1664. Because of this same change of owners and of names, and about the time of the creation of the Kissing Bridge (to which institution, in despite of its foreign genesis, the Dutch took most kindly), there came into existence also a rival English pleasure-garden that must have been a grievous thorn in Wolfert Webber's fat Dutch side.

The rival establishment, of which the proprietor was a loose fish named Richard Sacket, was over near the East River just north of where now is Franklin Square. It was known as the Cherry Garden — because of the cherry orchard which was one of its chief attractions — and the lane that ran beside it still exists, and still preserves its memory, in the grimy Cherry Street of the present day. There was a bowling-green in the garden, together with " other means of diversion,"

declare the chronicles; but what these other
means of diversion were, the chroniclers—following the annoying example of reticence set by He-
rodotus—do not tell.  However, without regard
to their respective attractions, the mere fact that
one of these gardens was Dutch and that the other was English was quite enough to break up the
New York pleasure-seekers of that period into
rival camps.  And so—until another generation
was grown and the bitterness of foreign conquest
was a little forgotten — there was Dutch merry-
making and patriotism on a basis of schnapps at
Wolfert Webber's; while at Richard Sacket's the
dominant English were gay in their own language
and drank toasts to Queen Anne and to the first
of the Georges in their favorite West India rum.

Possibly because of the succession of the
House of Hanover, certainly at about that period,
and from that period onward, the garden habit
of New-Yorkers, already well fixed, became very
much intensified.  In the early years of the eighteenth century another rival to Wolfert Webber
established himself almost directly over that
worthy man's nose—that is to say, on the top of
the near-by Catimut's Hill; down on Crown
Street (the Liberty Street of the present day)
was Barberrie's Garden; over near the shore of
the North River (as may be seen on Lyne's map
of 1729) was the Bowling Green Garden, which a
little later was renamed Vauxhall; in this same
vicinity, about the year 1750, Ranelagh (whereof
I have written elsewhere) was evolved from the

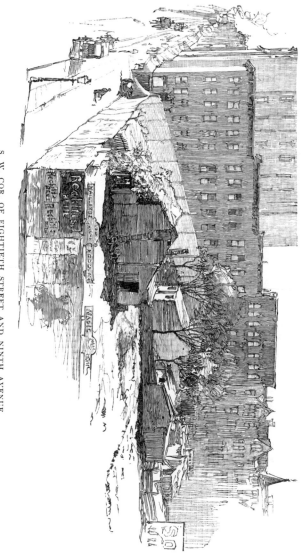

S. W. COR. OF EIGHTIETH STREET AND NINTH AVENUE

homestead of Colonel Rutgers; Brannan's Garden
was established out on the Greenwich Road, to
the northward of Lispenard's Meadows, about
the year 1765; before the end of the century
Byram's Garden—subsequently known as Corri's,
and as the Mount Vernon Garden—adorned the
hill-top above where now is the crossing of Leonard Street and Broadway; to this same neighborhood Contoit's New York Garden was transferred
(from opposite to the City Hall Park) about the
year 1809 and there continued its vivacious existence for a term of forty years: during which
period Castle Garden (a garden only by courtesy,
being actually a stone fort surrounded by water)
ran through nearly the whole of its brilliant career;
while Niblo's, in the year 1828, began the life as a
garden that as a theatre continues even until this
present day. Keeping together the whole of this
long chain—whereof many links have not been
named—was the Atlantic Garden, as it was called
in its latter days, at the lower end of Broadway:
a place of entertainment that began life as the
garden of the old tavern known successively as
Krieger's, Burns's Coffee House, and the King's
Arms, and that maintained its easy-going and
genial existence from a time only a little later
than the founding of New Amsterdam until less
than five-and-thirty years ago.

Excepting only Castle Garden—the great glory
of which as a place of amusement has been un-
fairly dimmed by its degenerate squalor in later
times as an emigrant dépôt—the most brilliant

of all of these technically rural resorts was Vauxhall : whereof the record, though relating to different sites and to many different managements,
practically is continuous for considerably more
than one hundred years.

The beginning of this pleasuring - place, as I
have written above, was very early in the eighteenth century and under the name of the Bowling Green.   At that time it was far away in the
country, being a leasehold on the Church Farm;
while still in its prime the city grew out to it ;
and in its last days this once-fashionable resort,
its garden sold off in building lots, was sunk to
the level of a low groggery (standing at the corner of Warren and Greenwich streets) in what
then was the shabbiest part of the town.   However, before this dismal destiny overtook the
primitive Vauxhall, its respectable name seems
to have been transferred to a Vauxhall which
Mr. Valentine affirms was established by one
Delacroix in the year 1798 on Bayard's Mount,
in the old Bayard homestead ; and thence was
shifted, five or six years later, to the ultimate
Vauxhall: which had the good-fortune not only
to lead a respectable life, but to pass out of existence in a genteel obscurity with no blot upon its
name.

This last Vauxhall Garden—which for half a
century had been a real garden wherein Jacob
Sperry, a Swiss, grew flowers and fruit for the
New York market—became a pleasure-garden in
the year 1803: when Sperry, waxing old in his

NINETY-FIFTH STREET AND PARK AVENUE

gentle calling, sold the property to Mr. Astor,
and when Mr. Astor leased it for one-and-twenty
years (according to Valentine) " to a Frenchman
named Delacroix, formerly a keeper of the Vauxhall on the old Bayard estate," who turned the
green-house into " a handsome saloon " and transferred to the establishment his own capable man
agement and the long-popular name.

The venture was rather a daring one, for the
garden was more than a mile out of town on the
Bowery Road; that is to say, was just south of
what now is Astor Place and what then was beginning to be called Art Street though still cur-
rently known as Monument Lane. However, it
became immediately a fashionable resort ; and
when, a little later, the theatre was built and
the garden — already " provided with summer-
houses for the accommodation of company "—
was " adorned with busts and statues," all the
town flocked to it, and its prosperity was assured
for a long term of years.

Certain sprightly friends of mine, at least two
decades younger than the present century, remember well this gallant garden in its later
days ; and they protest that what with its dazzle
of lamps in the arbors and shrubbery, and its fire-
works and fire - balloons, and its music, and the
performances of that killing comedian Twaits in
such dashing bits as " The Agreeable Surprise "
—to say nothing of the palate-tickling things to
eat and to drink which there abounded—'twas as
gay a place of recreation as was to be found at

that period of an evening anywhere in the civ-
ilized world.

These young ancients—who are by no means
too old to go for a frolicsome evening to El Do-
rado, yet who remember so freshly this other
pleasure-garden that to the present generation is
buried figuratively beneath the sands of time, and
literally beneath the far-extending walls of the
Astor Library—bring us very close to our point
of departure: and so emphasize the continuity of
our rural pleasure-places from the placid Dutch
period even until the present day. For this garden which they vividly remember had its beginning while Wolfert Webber's and Richard Sacket's gardens still flourished, and while Dutch
schnapps and the more subtle spirit of Dutch
patriotism still held out bravely against English
aggression and English rum.

NINETY-SEVENTH STREET NEAR PARK AVENUE

## NEW AND OLD NEW YORK

EVEN down in the densely-built region between what used to be Lispenard's Meadows and what used to be Love Lane—that is to say, between the present Canal Street and the present Twenty-first Street — there still may be found many ancient wooden houses which survive from the time when all this region was open country, broken only by a few dwellings scattered along the central highway and along the half-dozen minor roads and lanes.

A few of these wooden veterans have been wheeled around on their timber toes to the lines of the City Plan, and face boldly upon the existing streets—as in the case of the little houses on the southeast corner of the Sixth Avenue and Eleventh Street. But, as a rule, land fronting on any street is too valuable to be encumbered by such poverty-stricken remnants of an earlier time, and the wooden buildings are tucked away modestly in the centres of the blocks—where they are to be come at only by adventuring into the twilight depths of tunnel-like alleyways or up narrow courts. For instance, in the rear of No. 112 Ninth Avenue—on the line of an old country road whereof the very name, if it ever had one, is forgotten—there is in use as a dwelling a house

which was built not less than fifty years ago,
when all about it was open fields; and between
Sixteenth and Seventeenth streets, west of the
Sixth Avenue, there survives in the centre of the
block a whole row of wooden houses—on the line
of the old Southampton Road, and once known
as Paisley Place—which date from the yellow-
fever summer of 1822.

Certain mild-mannered elderly people, folk of
kindly natures and gentle antiquarian tastes, have
a feeling of warm friendliness for these remnants
of what hereabouts (where all is so very new) we
are pleased to style antiquity. For such there
is pleasure in speculating upon how each little
house came into being in the open country years
ago; and upon how the city grew out toward
them all, and then around them, until at last they
fairly were buried in its heart. For the whole
process seems remote and curious, and therefore
is permeated by a delicately agreeable flavor of
romance.

And yet, in point of fact, one has only to take
a train on the elevated railway, and so jog northward (if so bustling a word as jog may be applied
to the elevated-railway service) for three or four
miles, and one finds to-day precisely the conditions of open country and wooden houses and an
advancing city which obtained between Lispenard's Meadows and Love Lane a long lifetime
ago. In other words, just as comparative ethnol-
ogists study primitive types in existing races of a
low order (such as the Maoris and other savages

PARK AVENUE AND NINETY-SEVENTH STREET

who lack intellectuality and dress mainly in bad smells), so may comparative sociologists study very accurately in the upper half of this island at the present day what has been going on in the lower half of it for the past two hundred and fifty years. Constantly the line of substantial buildings is advancing northward, and along the whole length of this line, from river to river, the old constantly is displaced by or is obscured by the new. Did the mass of brick and stone move forward with a uniform front, the new simply would overwhelm the old, and that would be the end of it. But the advance is made precisely as an army marches into an enemy's country: with a light skirmish-line thrown out far ahead to feel the way; with substantial columns of reconnoissance supporting the skirmishers; and in the rear of all the solid masses of the main force—with the coming of which last the country definitely is subdued.

It is the beginning of the conquest that is interesting—the period between the arrival of the skirmishers and the coming of the supporting force; that is to say (to drop the metaphor), the period during which the houses of brick and stone are coming into a straggling existence on the lines of the City Plan, but while yet many of the little wooden houses still stand at hopeless odds with the new thoroughfares—testifying to the lines of country roads which have disappeared beneath a gridironing of city streets—and while still remain wide stretches of open country across which are far outlooks to the wooded heights beyond the North River, and away eastward to the Long Island hills.

Nowhere on the whole northern front of the advancing city is the imminently impending ploughing under of the old by the new accented with such dramatic intensity as in the vicinity of Ninety-seventh Street and Park Avenue: where a score or more of little houses, surviving from a primitive rural time, stand close under the shadow of the stately armory of the Eighth Regiment and are pressed upon closely by solidly built blocks of handsome dwellings of almost literally the present day.

None of these little houses is entitled to much respect on the score either of age or of personal dignity. When the Commissioners' map was completed, eighty years ago, the only building in this immediate vicinity was the Rhinelander farm-house, on the line of the present Ninety-first Street between the Second and Third avenues. From that point northward to 104th Street, on the borders of the Harlem marsh, and between the line of the present Fifth Avenue and the East River, there were only three other houses all told. None of these wooden buildings, therefore, is more than eighty years old, and probably none of them is much turned of forty. As for their personality, for the most part they are no more than shanties. Yet, as the city grows around them, they perfectly illustrate the process by which houses of a nobler sort in the lower part of the island have been surrounded;

WEST OF CENTRAL PARK

and so, for a longer or shorter period, have been preserved. Half a century from now such of them as then may chance to remain extant will put on, no doubt, vastly important airs (as do also certain vulgar humans under like circumstances), for no better reason than that they have attained to unusual years. Yet will they then to some extent deserve respectful consideration, because—even as a personally unimportant trilobite throws light upon an unknown epoch—they then will serve to illustrate a vanished age.

In the meantime these shanties of low degree give a touch of the picturesque to a neighborhood that otherwise—save for the redeeming glory of the armory—would be an ill-made compromise between the unkempt refuse of the country and the dull newness of the advancing town. Once they must have occupied a very picturesque site, but that point in their favor long since was lost. They are clustered together on what anciently was a hill-side sloping down to the East River directly above Hell Gate. But now the streets brought to grade above them have left them in a hollow, and half a mile of solidly built-up city cuts off the old outlook eastward: across the wild rush of the Hell Gate waters swirling about the Frying-pan and the Gridiron and seething in the Pot. Around these shabby, down-at-heel dwellings, and even over some of them, go frisking wise-looking bearded goats in the gravely grotesque fashion peculiar to their kind. In one of the doorways a very bandy-legged bull-dog sometimes may be seen. Quite the most respectable of all their inhabitants is a staid gray cat.

Presently the whole of this queer little congregation will have disappeared: being hidden by enclosing lines of brick dwellings—as is the old house on the Eighth Avenue, on the line of the forgotten country road; or, what is more probable, being uprooted completely—as was the similar group of small wooden houses which stood, not much more than half a century ago, on what is now the block between Fifteenth and Sixteenth streets just east of Union Square.

As for the Eighth Regiment Armory—standing commandingly on a brave crest of rock between the East River and the valley in which anciently were the head-waters of Harlem Creek, and regnant over all this portion of the town—it is so noble a structure that only its accessibility saves it from becoming a place of pilgrimage and from acquiring an honorable renown. After the Palace of the Popes, the chief building in Avignon is the Castle of Saint André, over in the Ville Neuve. Travellers journey far that they may see this castle, and its fame is spread over the world. But here at our very doors is almost its counterpart—only on a far grander scale: the New York castle is fully twice as big as the castle at Ville Neuve d'Avignon—and there are thousands of New-Yorkers who do not even know that it exists!

In the same latitude as the Park Avenue shanties, but in a longitude about one minute farther west—that is to say, near the intersection of the

A BIT ON THE BOULEVARD

Bloomingdale Road with Ninety-eighth Street—
the process of burying a whole row of wooden
houses in the heart of a city block now is in progress: the same process that was completed when
the erection of the brick dwellings on Seventeenth
Street shut in Paisley Place, forty or more years
ago.

Nowadays the Bloomingdale Road is called
the Boulevard—an exquisitely absurd name for a
street which has no more to do with fortifications,
actual or extinct, than it has to do with the moon.
On its western side, between the lines of the present Ninety-second and Ninety-sixth streets, there
was a hamlet of a dozen houses in the early years
of the present century; and near by, on the actual line of the present Ninety-ninth Street, stood
St. Michael's Church. Some of these buildings
still survive. Within the same limits many similar buildings—modest framed structures of two
stories, with a gabled attic; and here and there a
more pretentious dwelling of the villa type—have
been erected in later times; and, as yet, the modern brick houses are few. Thus are reproduced
in this region conditions almost identical with
the conditions which obtained sixty years ago in
the open, rolling country south of Greenwich Village—between, say, the present Leroy and Spring
streets—before the chain of hills known as the
Zandtberg was levelled, and while all that beautiful country-side was dotted with trig little houses
over which dominated such grand country-seats
as Tusculum and Richmond Hill.

It is a part of this scattered settlement that
now is in process of hiding: the row of wooden
houses standing in a narrow court extending south
from Ninety-eighth Street just west of the Tenth
Avenue—which court is a remnant of what once
was a lane running parallel with the Bloomingdale Road.   Already the enclosing wall to the
eastward has been erected, the solid line of houses
on the Tenth Avenue; and to the south the Ro-
man Catholic Church of the Holy Name of Jesus,
now building on Ninety-seventh Street, soon will
cut off another side.   When Ninety-eighth Street
and the absurd "Boulevard" shall have been built
upon, the cordon will be complete.   And then, if
the little houses in the meantime live on—and,
as they appear to be owned in severalty, this
very well may happen—the buried Paisley Place
at Seventeenth Street and the Sixth Avenue will
have an exact antitype four miles away to the
north.

Each of the localities to which attention here
has been drawn has individual features, but all of
them are typical.   They are representative in the
present of processes which we are disposed to
associate in our thoughts, but very erroneously,
wholly with the past.   Actually, to describe how
New York grew is only another way of describing
how New York grows: as may be proved to the
satisfaction of any person possessing serviceable
legs who will go a-walking in the upper portions
of this island with open eyes.

# INDEX

THE END